THE CLONED IDENTITY

Detective Inspector Roger Watson is getting nowhere. A forty-year-old spinster is in a coma in the hospital, and he is convinced she has been raped by the Reverend Thomas Wright. The investigation is floundering for lack of evidence, so the Inspector is persuaded to join forces with a scientist who claims to be able to download information directly from the human brain.

THE CLONED IDENTITY

David Hughes

ARTHUR H. STOCKWELL LTD
Torrs Park   Ilfracombe   Devon
Established 1898
www.ahstockwell.co.uk

British Library Cataloguing-in-Publication Data.
A catalogue record for this book is available
from the British Library.

This is an entirely fictional story,
and no conscious attempt has been made
to accurately record or recreate
any real-life events.

By the same author:
Purple Jade

ISBN 978-0-7223-4230-5
Printed in Great Britain by
Arthur H. Stockwell Ltd
Torrs Park   Ilfracombe
Devon

CHAPTER 1

"Joe, this had better be good," I snarled at the startled chap sitting behind the neat and tidy desk as I burst into the office, my dramatic entrance designed to convey my displeasure to anyone who witnessed it. I stopped in front of his desk and looked down at the man I had all but shouted at. "You do know this is the first break I've had since I started here?"

"Yes, boss; not my fault, honestly. The Chief Super insisted we recall you. I am sorry."

I looked at Joe. I could see the genuine hurt in his eyes.

"OK, Joe, give me ten minutes then come in."

Joe nodded and I turned and made my way to the cupboard in the corner which served as my office. I knew it was my office because it had my name on the door – no, not on a brass plate, not even on a plastic plate, but on a piece of card sellotaped on. A temporary measure, I had been assured on my first day – well, that was six months ago. Did I make a fuss about it? No, of course not. I had more important things on my mind, like catching criminals.

I entered my office and tried to slam the door shut, only the door wouldn't slam because it had been fitted with one of those damn automatic closing devices; so how was I expected to show what mood I was in? I rounded the bare desk, dropped into the swivel chair and swung round. Reaching inside my jacket, I unclipped the bleeper and threw it on the desk.

"Bloody bleepers!" I said to myself.

Talk about electronic tags for criminals! We were already fitted with them. I brought my fist down on the desk with a thud, which I truly hoped would be heard on the floor above. Angry? Why should I be angry? I mean, I had only spent the last six months pushing around bits of paper relating to really major crimes concerning lost cats and stolen video recorders and not forgetting shoplifters; then, the first day I have off, there I was in bed with this gorgeous women when the bloody bleeper went off and she leapt out of bed like a scalded cat and started running round the bedroom screaming for me to get dressed and get out. I finally calmed her down by chucking the duvet over her and sitting on top of her. When she had stopped shouting, mainly owing to the fact that she couldn't breathe, I let her up and asked what the hell was wrong. She told me her husband had a bleeper and when mine went off she thought he had come home and caught her. As you can imagine, the erotic moment had disappeared and with it my first chance of a leg-over in six months. So I was really happy. I was just acting mad to keep Joe on his toes. Blasted thing! I snatched the bleeper off the desk, opened a drawer, chucked it in and slammed the drawer closed.

A dark sadness came over me as I leant back and surveyed my cupboard. To think six months ago I was in a proper office in Scotland Yard, the hub of the Metropolitan Police, famous throughout the world! I was part of a thriving team with plenty of manpower, dealing with proper crimes. I had been looking at a brilliant career. I was well in with the right people.

I had made detective inspector three years before most would have done; then it had all come crashing down, all because of a woman – a woman called Sylvia, to be exact. Now, Sylvia had been left on her own at home while her power-mad husband had gone off chasing his career. So there was this woman, older than me, at a time in her life when she needed to be reminded that she was still attractive and desirable. So along came me, young, virile and hungry. I had already had more than my fair share of women, but Sylvia was something else. You couldn't get bored with her. Every time we got it together, she treated it as though it was going to be her last time and she made sure she enjoyed every minute – no lying back and faking it with her! She wouldn't let me go until she was satisfied – and I mean *satisfied*. Sometimes she would need three or four orgasms before she was happy. We went through all the fantasies she had stored up during her life, plus some more she had dreamt up since we met. I had never felt so satisfied with sex in my life before. She really drained me; and I felt sorry for her husband, who probably never knew what he had been missing. Not only that, but he was the sort who would probably go out and pay some tom for what his wife could give him if he only knew how to treat her.

But all good things have to come to an end, and of course her husband found out – and no, he didn't appreciate the fact that I had been doing him a favour, looking after his wife while he got on with his career. And I soon found out that it had not been a wise move on my part to sleep with the wife of my boss. He knew more influential people than I did, and my career took a nosedive. I was transferred out to the very fringes of the Met, to Milton. Milton was a dump – a sort of retirement home for has-beens where a major crime was a lost pension book or a missing cat. It was slowly driving me bonkers.

My self-commiseration was suddenly interrupted by a meek tap at the door and Joe came in holding a folder in his hand.

"Sit down, Joe." I gestured to the only other chair this cupboard had space for. "OK, what's the flap about?" I asked.

"Well, boss, we have had a serious assault, possibly a rape."

"Good grief, Joe! I know that's a bit unusual for round here, but surely it could have waited till tomorrow."

"Yes, boss, I agree. I had everything in hand, but apparently the Bishop plays golf with the Chief and—"

"Hold on. Are you saying someone's raped the Bishop or his wife?"

"No, boss," said Joe with half a grin, "not even his daughter – that's if he has got one. No, it is one of his flock. She is very prominent in the local church circle, fund-raising, flower-arranging – that sort of thing. She also did a lot of charity work – not the usual sort of woman who gets raped, I would have thought."

"Joe, let me tell you I've dealt with many rape cases and there's no such thing as a 'usual sort'. It can happen to any female; all she has to be is in the wrong place at the wrong time. Most rapes are done on impulse and are not premeditated."

"Sorry, boss. I didn't mean—"

"That's all right," I replied, trying to sound nice.

The pain caused by my reprimand showed in Joe's face. Joe was a good 'by the book' copper, and had he had more flair he would have gone higher than detective sergeant. As it was he seemed happy to stay where he was, to see out the three years to his pension.

"So, Joe, what have you done so far?"

"Well, boss, it's all in there."

He passed over the folder, which I took and put in front of me unopened.

"I'll read that later. Tell me in your own words."

"Right. Well, when the call came in I went straight to the scene and made sure the uniforms didn't throw all the evidence away. The victim had been taken to hospital before we arrived, so I sealed off the house and made sure nothing was moved. I was waiting for Mel and her crew to arrive to do the forensic, when this chap turned up and demanded to know what was going on and why we were there. Anyway, he became quite upset. I asked if he was the husband or a relative, but he became really abusive and cleared off. Later I got a radio call from the Chief; I was to report back to him immediately. So I rushed back and he carpeted me – had a right go at me – and ordered me to find you and hand the case over."

I looked at Joe. His eyes were a bit misty as he stared down at the desk; it showed what a 'conscience' copper he was. I knew without looking in the folder in front of me that it would be spot on with facts which were facts and not opinions or presumptions.

"So what was it about, Joe? What did the Chief say exactly?"

"Well, you know I mentioned that chap who appeared while I was down at the scene?"

I nodded.

"It turned out he was the local vicar. I didn't know that at the time because he wasn't wearing a dog collar and he didn't identify himself."

"Go on," I said.

"The vicar – he went and rang the Bishop and told him I had been deliberately obstructive and rude. So the Bishop phoned the

Chief and I got a right rollicking — Ah, sorry, boss," he stammered as I looked at him in surprise. That was the first time I had heard Joe swear since I had been there.

"Don't worry, Joe. That's the way it goes sometimes." I opened the folder and flicked through the pages. "Looks like you've done a good job here, Joe – a good job." I hoped my praises made up for the way he had been treated. "Right, Joe, take me through what's in here," I said, tapping the folder.

"Right, boss. The victim, a Miss Susan Wood, spinster, aged round about forty, lives on her own. That's what we have found out so far. It would appear that she was attacked yesterday evening or during the night. She was found by a friend, Mrs Vivian Thomas, at about nine o'clock this morning. The previous evening Miss Wood had been at Mrs Thomas's house and they had agreed that Mrs Thomas would call for Miss Wood and they would go to the vicarage together. They had an appointment with the vicar. When Mrs Thomas arrived at Miss Wood's, she found the front door ajar. The lock had the latch on. She rang the bell and called out. Getting no reply, she looked in the back garden. Apparently Miss Wood couldn't open the back door – the bolts were stuck or the door warped. I've checked that out and I can't open it; so she always used the front door when she went into the back garden. Mrs Thomas then entered the house and looked downstairs. Finding no one, she then went upstairs and found Miss Wood apparently asleep in her bed. She tried to wake her, but found she couldn't; so she called her doctor."

"Not an ambulance?" I asked.

"No, boss. She said she seemed so normal that she thought perhaps she had taken a sleeping pill. She had done that before, so Mrs Thomas wasn't too worried. The Doctor arrived and gave her a quick once-over. He noticed some bruises on the side of her neck, and the way she was lying was odd, he said."

"Odd, Joe? In what way?"

"Well, he said she looked as if someone had put her in the bed. The position she was in and the way the bedclothes were arranged made it seem like someone had laid her out."

"You mean laid out like in an undertaker's?"

"Yes, that's it, boss. Anyway, he couldn't wake her so he called for an ambulance first and then us."

"He only called us because of the marks on her neck?"

"No, not quite. While he was waiting for the ambulance he checked her over and found some more bruises, and he was convinced she must have been attacked in some way."

"So what you are saying, Joe, is that we don't know for sure if she was attacked."

"She was attacked, boss. I had a call from the hospital just a minute ago, and they agree that it looks like a sexual assault took place. Force appears to have been used."

"Did they say how she was? Can she make a statement yet?"

"No – there's another problem. She's in some sort of coma. They're running some tests, but they can't tell us any more until the morning."

"What about relatives – next of kin?"

"Mrs Thomas says the only one she knows of is an uncle who lives up north. I found an address for an Edward Mark in Tolchester. I've sent a fax to the local nick and asked them to inform him of what's happened."

"Well, Joe, it doesn't look like you have left me much to do."

My praise met with a shrug, which said, "Just doing my job, boss."

Just then the phone rang. I answered: "Yes, sir, I am with him now." I listened for a few minutes then said, "Yes, of course, right away," and put the phone down.

"Chief?" Joe asked.

I nodded.

"How did he know I was in the building? Ah, never mind."

I looked at Joe. "It appears we are to go straight away and see your friend the vicar, and explain that we are moving heaven and earth on his behalf to solve this case and we won't be eating any bread or drinking any wine until we have."

Joe almost broke into a smile at my sarcasm.

"Is the house on the way to the vicar's?" I asked.

"Yes, boss, just round the corner."

"Good. We can drop in and I can get a feel of the place."

CHAPTER 2

We made our way to the garage and I asked Joe to drive so I could read through the file. Joe informed me when he turned into the road where Miss Wood lived. I stopped reading and looked at the houses.

It was a nice, quiet tree-lined road. The houses looked about fifty years old, built in blocks of four with a narrow gap between each block. The end houses in each block looked bigger because they had a bow window. The front gardens all looked neat and looked after, but boring in their similarity. Noting that there was no room for garages, I asked Joe if there was a rear service road. He said there was.

He pulled up outside number 48, which was the last house before a junction. As I got out of the car I could see the only difference between this and the other houses was the official tape across the front gate and the six-foot-six blue garden gnome wearing size-12 boots standing in the front garden. He rushed over to the gate and held the tape up for us.

"Lost your fishing rod?" I asked.

"Pardon, sir?" he said, looking puzzled.

I grinned at him as I walked past.

"I wonder how long he will take to work that out," I said quietly to myself.

"Sorry, sir – I didn't quite catch that," said Joe behind me.

"Oh, nothing, Joe – just thinking out loud."

I stopped about halfway down the path and looked up at the house. The green and white paintwork was in poor repair, but I could see that the windows and the curtains were clean. I looked at the front door. Despite the faded green paintwork, the brass letter box and the red tiles in the small porch looked freshly polished. I noted that the path to the side of the house led to a gate set in a dark creosoted, trellis-topped fence – the way to the back garden, I presumed. We carried on up to the front door, which I could see was ajar. I could see from the powder smudges where the forensic boys had been.

Using one finger, I pushed open the door and stepped into a narrow hallway. I could see it was clean, despite the darkness.

"There's a front room, back room and kitchen down here; three bedrooms and bathroom upstairs," Joe volunteered.

Without looking at him, I nodded in response.

I stood with my back to the front door. The stairs were on my right, the doors to the two reception rooms were on my left and the kitchen straight ahead. The hall was decorated with a faded flower-patterned wallpaper, which fitted in neatly between the picture rail and skirting board, both of which had been stained or varnished in some bygone age. I looked up the stairs, the narrow flimsy-looking stair carpet clamped into position by dark, heavy stair rods. The only thing missing from this time warp was the ticking of a clock.

"Upstairs, was it?"

"Yes, boss – front bedroom," answered Joe.

We made our way upstairs, the wood creaking in protest at our combined weight.

The small landing was lighter than the hall downstairs. Someone had painted the doors, skirting board and picture rails white. I could see from the way the paint had peeled here and there that the painter had slapped the paint straight on top of the varnish. Here and there were traces of forensic powder.

"That door there, boss." Joe pointed to the second door on my right.

Using my finger, I pushed the door open and stepped into a sad-looking room. Although the curtains were pulled right back, it was still dark. All the furniture was old-fashioned dark oak. There was nothing in the room to reflect the light. The room felt silent and lifeless. It seemed as though any sign of life in this room would be absorbed by the dark and lost for ever. I walked over to the bay window and confronted the heavy-looking dressing table. I looked at my reflection in the oval mirror, the image tarnished by the damage caused by age and damp to the mirror backing. I toyed with a chrome-handled brush-and-comb set resting in a glass tray, and reflected that my mother had a similar set on her dressing table, yet I had never seen her using it. I picked up the brush, and realised how unyielding it was. The head was heavy; the handle by comparison was slender and light. It had obviously been designed from the aesthetic rather than the practical point of view. Sighing, I carefully replaced the brush and turned round. The bed was between me and Joe. I looked it over – dark-wood headboard and footboard; the naked mattress looked old and lumpy. The room had a cell-like atmosphere – not a prison cell, but a monk's or nun's cell. It wasn't a happy room; it was a room for a purpose. I couldn't imagine it had ever heard the sound of laughter or the cries of pleasure of a couple loving. The floor was covered in cold, dark lino, although there was a dull rectangle by the side of the bed where I assumed a rug must have been before it was spirited away along with the bedding by Mel and her crew. They would caress it with modern technology into giving up any secrets it might hold.

I looked up at Joe. "A very sad house, Joe – more like a shrine than part of someone's life."

He shrugged his shoulders.

"Right," I said, breaking the silence, "let's go and see your mate."

We left the house, pulling the front door closed. I told the PC to make sure it was all locked up before he left; and I nearly asked if he had worked out about the fishing rod, but thought better of it.

It took only about ten minutes to get to the vicarage. The church was a simple barn-like building. It had no tower or steeple – just a pile of red bricks. We pulled into the small gravelled car park, and from there I followed Joe through a gap in the dense, manicured hedge. The gravel path was wide enough for us to walk side by side. The vicarage was built of the same red bricks as the church; the windows were leaded, as if to add an air of respectability to the blandness of the walls. The end of the path was blocked by two steps, which led up to a shallow porch and a wide, wooden front door furnished with heavy, black wrought-iron fittings (apart from the doorbell, which was of highly polished brass).

Joe gave the bell some exercise and we waited. We couldn't wait on the top step as it wasn't wide enough. I wondered if it had been made like that so visitors had to wait on the lower step so that when the door opened they would be looking up at the vicar, to make sure they knew who was boss – just a thought.

The door suddenly swung open and the vicar stood there, tall and well built, with whitish wavy hair, brown eyes and thick lips. He was wearing a grey suit and glasses. I absorbed his details automatically as I asked if he was the Reverend Wright. Thereon he asked who we were. We identified ourselves and flashed our cards, and he said he was indeed the Reverend Wright. He apologised for his abruptness, saying that we looked just like a couple of book salesmen.

"Please do come in," he said, standing back.

We entered a hall which was completely the opposite of the one we had just left: it was light, wide and untidy, but homely. The vicar closed the front door and asked us to follow him.

He led us into what must have been his study, which made me very conscious of my limited knowledge of religion. I had always thought there was only one book on religion and that was the Bible, but here we had wall-to-wall religious books crammed into solid wooden bookcases. The vicar made his way to his desk – and what a desk! It looked as though it must weigh a couple of tons. It was huge and covered in polished leather. He asked if we would like to sit down, pointing to the two handsome leather chairs in front of the desk. He waited until we were seated before he sat down. It was very evident as soon as he sat down that there had been some arranging, as we were clearly lower than he was – not much, but just enough to give him the advantage.

I explained to the vicar that we were investigating the attack on Miss Wood, and he asked if we had any news.

"It really is a dreadful business – quite shocking. Not the sort of thing you expect round here."

"Yes, Joe – Sergeant Gibson – said you were upset."

"Upset! My good man, when a friend – a dear, dear lady who wouldn't hurt a fly – is violated in her own home, I think I have a right to be upset, don't you?"

I looked at him for a few seconds, then said, "Reverend, I take it you know Miss Wood quite well?"

"Yes, of course. She was just as much a personal friend as a willing helper."

I nodded. "Well, be assured we will do everything we can to solve this case as quickly as possible. I myself was recalled from holiday. I can understand the distress this has caused you, but it would be helpful if we could ask you some questions – get some idea of Miss Wood's background."

"Yes, of course I must do all I can to help; we all must."

"Is it all right if Sergeant Gibson here makes some notes?"

He nodded.

"Can you tell us if Miss Wood had any male friends or enemies?"

"Enemies? Are you mad? Susan was a saint – everyone liked her."

"Not quite everyone," I said.

He glared at me and said, "No, I suppose not."

"So you don't know anyone who might wish her any harm?"

He shook his head.

"What about men friends?"

Again he shook his head.

"Has she mentioned that anyone had been pestering or bothering her lately – nuisance phone calls, that sort of thing?"

"No, not that I can recall," he answered.

"So when was the last time you saw her?"

"That would be yesterday, around lunchtime. She called in to tell me she would be coming round this morning with Mrs Thomas."

"How did she seem to you?"

"She was smiling, happy – just as she always was."

"Going back to this morning, can you tell me exactly what happened?" I sat back in my chair.

"As I've said, I was expecting her to come round about eight thirty. She was always prompt. I waited until about ten to nine;

then I tried to phone her. But there was no answer, so I decided to pop round – it's only round the corner. When I got there, the place was swarming with police – it gave me quite a fright – and the sergeant here [he scowled at Joe] wouldn't let me in or tell me what was going on."

"That's standard procedure," said Joe, butting in. "If you had said who you were—"

"But I told you who I was!" The vicar was now interrupting Joe.

"No, sir, I don't think you did," replied Joe.

I thought I'd better intervene before it developed into a full-scale row: "What did you do then?" I asked.

The vicar turned towards me and gave me a look of disapproval, as though irritated by my calling him to order. "Why – why, I came back here and finished the proofs of the church magazine. That was why Miss Wood and Mrs Thomas were coming round: they were suppose to be helping me. As it was, I was lucky I finished before the deadline. I then took them straight down to Kay's in the High Street. On my return I phoned the police station and met with the same response as I'd had from the Sergeant here." He again glared at Joe, who shifted uneasily in his seat. "So I phoned my Bishop and told him how I had been treated; then a little later he phoned me back and told me he had found out what had happened. I really couldn't believe it. How could such a thing happen right here on my own doorstep? Whatever next!"

"There's nothing else you can think of?" I asked.

"No, I think that's about everything."

"Well, if anything else springs to mind, perhaps you can call me?" I passed over one of my cards, and he took it, looked at it, then put it on his desk. "Well, thank you for your time. We won't take any more of your time."

We all stood up. I started to turn towards the door and stopped.

"I am sorry for the way you have been treated, but, as this case is so unusual for this area, the officers involved were probably overzealous."

He acknowledged my apology with a nod.

16

The three of us made our way back to the front door without speaking further. Joe and I stepped outside and I quickly turned back to face the vicar, who was about to close the door.

"Oh, by the way, Miss Wood – she is still in a coma, but her condition is stable. I just thought you might want to know."

He gave me a look which made me think that if he had been into black magic I would have been stoking the fires below.

I turned away before he could slam the door. Joe and I were a good couple of yards away before I heard the door close with a thud.

"That was a bit cruel, boss."

"A bit cruel, Joe? Did you notice all the sorrow and concern, yet he never once asked how she was – a bit strange, don't you think?"

"Unless he had just been on to the hospital and already knew."

"No, Joe, I don't think so; I think he would have mentioned it."

We covered the rest of the distance back to the car in silence.

On our way back to the station I said to Joe, "What did you make of the vicar?"

"Nothing really, boss. I am not a churchgoer myself, so I've never had much to do with vicars. I mean, they seem to do a good job – no harm in them, I suppose."

"Well, I didn't like him, Joe – not one little bit. Has he been here a long time?"

"No, about four years according to the Thomas woman. I couldn't stop her talking. I think she gave me the complete local history going back twenty years. She did say she preferred the previous vicar. Apparently he was married with a family and he fitted in much better."

"So this one is not married, then?"

"No, that's right, which makes it awkward."

"Awkward? How?" I asked.

"Well, according to the Thomas woman they had got used to dealing with the vicar's wife; this chap sees everything from a man's point of view, so it leads to a bit of friction and gossip."

"Gossip? What about?" I asked.

"You name it. Apparently, there has been talk among the women that he paid too much attention to Miss Wood."

"Jealous were they?" I asked.

"Well, you know what women are like, boss."

'Yes, only too bloody well! I'll swear it was one of Sylvia's friends who grassed on us,' I thought to myself.

CHAPTER 3

Back behind my desk I eyed the pile of folders which had appeared in my absence. Then I scooped them up and dumped them in the 'pending' tray. Well, I had a priority case now, didn't I?

My phone rang. It was the Chief, wanting to know my progress. He finished the call by telling me he could ask the Met for some help if he considered we needed it.

'Thanks a lot!' I thought. 'Thanks for the warning.'

Joe came in with the coffees.

"I've just had a word with Melanie. The only thing she can tell us so far is that it definitely wasn't a break-in."

"Is that all she can come up with?" I asked.

"That's all at the moment, boss. She thinks it will be another day at least before she has any more."

"Blast! How the hell can we progress with what we've got so far, which, Joe, when you look at it amounts to sod all? Sit down, Joe, and let's see if we can enlighten ourselves. We know that our suspect didn't need to break in, so that could mean he was known to Miss Wood. Perhaps he had been in the house before and had obtained a key in some way."

"He could have already been in the house waiting."

"Yes, that's another possibility, Joe. I want you to go back and have a good look round again; look to see if any work has been done recently – you know, cooker repaired, decorating, that sort of thing. Look for any tradesmen's cards. Check the parish magazine – you sometimes get local tradesmen advertising in them."

"OK, boss, I'll get straight on to that in the morning."

"Now, another thing, Joe: when she was found she was wearing a dressing gown as well as a nightdress, so she must have been ready for bed when she was attacked."

Joe piped in: "Or she could have been already in bed and got up. If she was in bed and someone rang her doorbell, she would have put the dressing gown on before she went down."

"OK, Joe, point taken. So let's agree that someone rang her doorbell, and that she was either in or ready for bed. She went to the front door, opened it—"

Joe piped in again: "According to the Thomas woman she was most careful about locking up, and kept the chain on."

"OK, let's assume she had the chain on. She opened the door, saw who it was, closed the door and took the chain off and let them in. Now, who would she know or trust to let in at that time of night?"

"There's the other possibility I mentioned, boss: that he was already in the house. He could have taken the chain off as he left."

"We've got too many ifs, Joe. We need a lot more facts. In your report you said she got home at about eight."

"Well, that was an estimate, boss. After they left the vicar's they went to afternoon tea at the WI – that's in the church hall. They left about five thirty and went back to Mrs Thomas's, where they stayed until Miss Wood left at seven thirty to walk home by herself. It takes about twenty minutes, so she should have arrived home about eight."

"We need to confirm that time, Joe, just in case she stopped off anywhere. Can we check if she did this visit on a regular basis? Someone could have clocked her. Oh, this Thomas woman – does she have a husband?"

"No, boss, he died three years ago."

"Also check with Mrs Thomas if she has noticed anyone lately taking an interest in the Wood woman. What about work – did she have a job?"

"No, she didn't work. Again according to Thomas, she once worked at the bank in James Street, but about five years ago a distant aunt left her enough to live on. She was very glad to give her job up."

"Why was that?" I asked.

"Well, the bank was changing over to computers and Miss Wood was finding it difficult to cope with the modern technology."

"I see. You didn't find a will at the house, did you?"

"Well, no, boss, but she's not dead, is she?"

"No, not as far as I know, but perhaps she was meant to be if she has money. In my experience, money is the motive behind most crimes. What about the uniforms on door-to-door – anything there?"

"I've only had a quick look at the notes – nothing unusual. The woman opposite thinks she saw a man walking a dog about seven, but no one so far saw Miss Wood come home."

"No, I expect they were all glued to the TV." We sat quietly for a few minutes, then I said, "I'll see Gibbard before I go and see if he can lend me a WPC tomorrow. I can get her to visit the WI members – find out what the gossip is. They're more likely to talk to a woman. And another thing, Joe: find out if the church is running any special programmes."

"In what way, boss?"

"Oh, you know, help the ex-con or down-and-outs, run soup kitchens – that sort of thing. If Miss Wood had been helping someone lately, and they knocked on her door, she might have let them in rather than turn them away. See if you can find out if she's been on holiday or on any courses lately – anywhere she might have met someone. Get a list of everyone she might have been in contact with. See if she was on any committees or in the church choir. I don't want all we know about Miss Wood to have come from Mrs Thomas. That's probably a biased source. I want to know her, Joe; I want to know her life pattern."

"Phew! OK, boss, but I think we are going to need some help."

"Don't worry, Joe – I'll get some help with the sorting and filing, and I'll ask the Chief to have Mike recalled off that course."

Joe gathered up his notes and left my office, and I reflected that there can't be many DIs around with just a sergeant and a DC as his entire staff.

The Chief readily agreed to recall Mike; he also allocated me a PC and a civilian typist. The PC, Jenkins, seemed keen enough, and I put him on collating the information we had already. I rang a few old mates in the Met to see if there had been any similar cases; I also checked on who had been released from prison recently. Both areas drew a blank.

I popped into the hospital mid-morning. I thought I might be able to get them to get a move on with their report – but no, the reports were not ready; and no, there was no change in Miss Wood's condition. I checked with the WPC, who looked bored out of her mind – but no, there had been no visitors. However, she told me the uncle had called and was travelling down, so I asked her to call in the moment he arrived.

On my way out I popped into the hospital shop and bought the thickest paperback they had and took it to the WPC. She thanked me with a lovely smile – well, she was quite nice. I had noticed her in the canteen, not that a DI would go out with a WPC – not from the same nick, anyway, but who knows? If I could solve this case, I could be transferred; I might even get a blessing from the Bishop and a discount on a burial plot.

Back at the office Joe was still out, Jenkins was hard at it and the typist was polishing her nails. I said some nice things to her, which made her blush, and I left her tapping away.

Back in my office I found the preliminary forensic report on my desk. I sat on the desk and read through the dozen or so pages. They were not really much help. In other words, there were no fingerprints of any known criminals.

I heard some voices and looked through the glass. Joe was back. I threw the report on the desk and went back into the main office. The typist spotted me coming and attacked her machine with a renewed vigour.

"How's it going?" I asked Joe.

"Oh, slowly, boss. I've bought another load of paperwork in for processing."

"Joe, I've got the prelim from Mel. It's not a lot of help."

"I know, boss. I bumped into her on the way in. She's a bit miffed. The Chief's been chasing her as well."

"Did she say when we would get the full report?"

"She reckons about five, boss."

I turned to go back to my office.

"Oh, Joe, I popped into the hospital, but there's no change. Let's see if we can aim for a meeting at six to chew over what we've got."

"OK, boss."

I spent the lunchtime in my office with a curled-up sandwich and a pint of milk. It wouldn't be right to be seen loitering in the canteen by one of the Chief's spies. The rest of the afternoon was spent on the phone or thinking – mostly about Sylvia, funnily enough. I found I missed her quite a lot, and I was toying with the idea of contacting her again – after all, we hadn't finished, not of our own free will, anyway. Perhaps I had better wait to see what happens with this case first.

At five fifteen both the hospital's and Mel's reports arrived. I read the hospital one first – that was certainly more interesting than Mel's – and I made some notes. I stood up and had a stretch.

I could see that Mike Dobson had arrived back. He was talking to Joe – moaning, no doubt, about being pulled off that nice cushy course he had wangled himself on to.

I settled down in my chair again, bang on six. Joe and Mike knocked and came in. I was glad to see that Mike had brought a chair with him for a change.

"Joe," I said, "ask Jenkins to join us. Make him feel wanted, then we might get some work instead of moans from him, and tell him to bring a chair."

While we waited I asked Mike how the course was going.

Presently Joe came back with Jenkins in tow, and there followed a shifting of chairs so they could all get in. Finally, when the movement and noise had stopped, I looked at Joe.

"Joe, perhaps you can start by filling us all in on what we know so far."

"OK, boss. The victim is a Miss Susan Wood, aged forty-four, spinster, lives on her own. She has no full-time employment and lives off an inheritance from an aunt. The only living relative we know about is an uncle who lives up north. Miss Wood is very active with her local church and supports many of the church activities. We do not know of any male friends, or enemies. She was apparently assaulted at home, possibly late evening. Money, chequebook and credit cards were all found in her handbag, so robbery has been ruled out."

"Not completely," I interrupted. "Could be something else was taken that we don't yet know about. Carry on, Joe."

"The attacker, we believe, was either known to the victim or was already waiting inside the house as there is no evidence of any forced entry. None of the neighbours noticed anything suspicious. The last person to see the victim before the attack was a Mrs Thomas, and that was at seven o'clock the same evening. It was Mrs Thomas who found the victim – that was about eight thirty the following morning. All the persons we have interviewed so far have given a similar picture of a cheerful, dedicated, caring person. And that's about it so far, boss."

"Thanks, Joe. Before we go any further I want to impress on you that this case is important – not just because of the nature of the crime, but because the Chief has a personal interest. So be warned and be on your guard. Now I've got the full forensic and hospital reports" – I tapped the folders in front of me – "I'll make sure you all get copies. The forensic doesn't help us very much, and the hospital report makes interesting reading, but again is not much help in solving the crime. I'll tell you the general details: The time of the attack is given at ten thirty to eleven. She was raped and had been a virgin. There are bruises to both sides of the throat, which indicate that the attacker grabbed her by the throat. The position of the bruises indicates that the attacker is taller than she is. She is five foot five, and the attacker is probably at least six foot. They think she was probably semi-conscious when she was forced on to the bed. There was no evidence, such as broken fingernails, etc., to indicate that she put up much of a fight, and Mel's report confirms that there were no signs of a struggle anywhere in the house. According to the hospital report, there was deep bruising on both sides of her hips at the rear, where he must have gripped her while he forced his way in. Judging by the severity of the bruising, he found it difficult, which suggests a man of limited sexual experience. Now the big surprise: no traces of semen were found anywhere, but they did find traces of lubricant – the sort used on condoms. This was found on the inside of both thighs, on her pubic hair and inside the vagina. The hospital think the coma was probably caused by shock and a lack of oxygen. There is evidence of smothering, but they don't think it was deliberate; it more than likely happened when he was lying on top of her, which again points to the man being considerably taller than she is."

I sat back in my chair with my hands clasped behind my head. Now, I know I am the only one in this room who has had previous experience of rape cases, but, let me tell you, this is the first time I've come across a rapist using a condom. Even when an assault is premeditated, the rapist is usually too busy and worked up to even think about a thing like that. One theory put forward on a course I went on was that rapists like to leave their mark on the victim, like animals putting scent marks around their territory. Now, you brainy lot, any ideas?"

"Well, boss, perhaps he was worried about catching something nasty, like Aids," said Jenkins.

"What about you, Mike?"

"Could be he knows about DNA."

"You mean, someone like a copper for instance?"

"I didn't mean that exactly, boss."

Jenkins shifted uneasily in his chair.

"But if it was a copper, boss, that might be why she let him in."

"That's right, Joe, but it could also be he has Aids or something nasty he doesn't want to pass on. If the DNA theory is correct, he is probably a person of intelligence, and he may be someone who has had previous experience."

"Do you mean he might have done it before, boss?"

"It's possible, Joe. Let's not discount it – not yet, anyway. OK, you can all see we have very little in the way of evidence. It doesn't matter how much theory we come up with, we can only solve this case with facts; so, starting tomorrow, Mike, you and Jenkins can go to the house and have a good look round – especially at that rear service road."

"Are we looking for anything in particular, boss?" asked Mike.

"Yes, Mike, you are. I want you to search the gardens, dustbins, hedges."

"What for, boss?" asked Mike, looking puzzled.

"The condom, Mike, the condom. He may have thrown it away as he left. Ask the neighbours – they may have found one in their front garden and disposed of it. Don't forget: be tactful. Condoms are still a mega embarrassment to some people."

Mike nodded.

"What about me, boss?"

"You, Joe? I want you to stay in the office. We need to sort out what we have already. OK, I can't think of anything else, so let's start fresh in the morning."

The meeting finished, and the three of them got up and juggled their way out of the office. Then my phone rang. I listened to the caller for a few minutes, then, putting the phone down, I shouted to Joe through the slowly closing door. He stuck his head round the door.

"That was the WPC at the hospital. The uncle, a Professor Edward Mark, has just turned up. Do we know anything about him?"

"Not a lot. Apparently he is some sort of egghead in research. Tolchester know him vaguely as there was some trouble at the lab where he works."

"Trouble? What sort of trouble?" I asked.

"They do experiments on animals, and some of the locals object to that sort of thing."

"Can you call in at the hospital on your way home and have a quick word with him. Usual stuff – when he last saw or heard from her."

"Yes, it's not out of my way."

"Don't forget to book it as overtime."

"OK, boss."

On the way down to the hospital, Joe thought back to the first time he had met DI Roger Watson. 'He doesn't just have a chip on his shoulder – more like a bloody great oak tree. He certainly makes it painfully obvious that he doesn't want to be here. Mind you, when I heard through the grapevine what had happened to him I couldn't really blame him. His record spoke for itself, and I am certainly glad he is with us now.'

At the hospital Joe located the WPC and she pointed him in the right direction. He stopped at the door she had pointed out and knocked and entered. There were two men in the room. The one wearing the white coat was talking to a well-built man, probably in his late forties. He was certainly colourful, wearing a multicoloured sports jacket with a spotted handkerchief and matching cravat. His small-check shirt looked as though it had been put on without ironing. They stopped their conversation as Joe walked over to them, and, in answer to their enquiring look, he introduced himself and flashed his ID. Joe held his hand out to the chap in the white coat.

"Dr Moore?" he said as they shook hands.

"Yes, but how—?"

"Did I know your name? I read it on your badge," Joe said, pointing to the name tag on his pocket.

He nodded and smiled.

Joe turned to the other man. "You must be Professor Mark."

"Yes, that's right."

He took Joe's hand and shook it vigorously. It struck Joe that he had very blue eyes.

Joe turned back to the Doctor and asked how Miss Wood was.

He told Joe there had been no change. "But, I was telling the Professor here, you can never tell in these cases," he added. "She could wake in the next few minutes, or she could go on for a long time. There is no way of knowing."

"I wonder, could I have a word with the Professor alone?"

"Yes, of course. I have work to do," said the Doctor. As he was leaving, he turned and said, "If you need me any time, the sister at the desk can bleep me."

They both nodded.

"Shall we sit down?" Joe suggested, pointing to the chairs. They both sat down opposite each other with a small square coffee table between them. Joe took out his notebook and received from him the nervous reaction he usually got whenever he did that, so Joe used his training to help him relax.

"Did you come by train?" Joe asked.

"Yes," he replied. Then he went on to display how nervous he was feeling by rambling on about how he didn't enjoy driving any more, and how things had changed. He said how startled he was, when he left the station, by the volume of noise and traffic.

Joe smiled. "Yes, I know what you mean."

After a few more minutes Joe soon had him ready. He opened his notebook.

"I would just like to ask you a few routine questions about your niece, if that's all right."

"Yes; I will help you all I can."

Joe smiled at him. They were old buddies now.

"When was the last time you saw your niece?"

"Let me see – that would be over a year ago. I came down to London for a lecture and we had dinner before I left."

"Did she seem all right then?"

"Yes, she seemed very happy and talked enthusiastically about her work at the church. She even talked me into making a donation." He smiled. "Made me write the cheque out on the spot, just in case I forgot when I got home."

"Have you had any contact with her since?" Joe asked.

"I spoke to her on the phone about three weeks ago."

"Why was that?" Joe asked.

He gave Joe a hard look.

"Oh, I don't mean to pry, but she could have phoned you because she was worried about something."

He relaxed and smiled.

"No, nothing like that. I phoned her to thank her for my birthday card. She never forgets – Christmas as well."

"How did she seem to you then?"

"Oh, the same as always. We chattered about the weather, state of the country, that sort of thing."

"Does she ever visit you?"

"No, no. My work, you see, involves using animals and Susan doesn't approve."

"Has she ever spoken to you of any problems relating to men?"

"Good God, no! Susan never looks at men in that way."

"No boyfriends, then?"

"I shouldn't think so. It was her parents, you see. Her father, he was a very strict man. God help any boy who came near her! Not only that, but she saw how he treated her mother – her father used to beat his wife regularly 'to cleanse her soul', as he put it. I don't know why she stayed with him so long. I begged Susan to leave home and start a life of her own, but she wouldn't leave her mother."

"What happened to them?"

"They were both killed in a car crash some seven years ago. That was their house that Susan lives in now. Have you seen it?"

Joe nodded.

"She hasn't changed a thing. I think she keeps it like that to remind her how her mother suffered." The Professor suddenly changed his mood, becoming more serious. He leant towards Joe. "Have you any idea who might have done this to her? I mean, why her, of all people?"

"No, we don't know who or why. As your niece is in a coma, we are working in the dark. We are collecting information and going through it, but it all takes time. If she wakes up, she can probably tell us who did it."

"You think it was someone she knows?"

"That is a possibility," Joe said; "but don't worry, Professor – we will catch him."

He sat back in his chair. "You know, on my way down in the train I thought about that."

"In what way?" Joe asked.

Sensing that the interview was finished, he closed his notebook.

"Well, the damage is done. Catching him – well, that won't help Susan. In fact, it could do her more harm. Her mind and body are already deeply scarred. Nothing can change that, but the added trauma of a court case, from what I've seen on TV and read in the papers, could be worse than the attack itself. I mean, how would that affect her?"

"I take your point, but suppose your niece could help us catch him, but didn't and he did it again – say, to a child. Suppose he killed his next victim. How would the knowledge that she could have prevented someone's death affect her? No, Professor, from what I've learnt about your niece, she would want him caught and put away."

The Professor's head had dropped on to his chest as he listened to Joe's sermon.

"Are you staying locally?" Joe asked as a way of changing the subject.

"Yes, at the Wessex." He perked up a bit.

"Yes, I know it – nice place."

Joe got to his feet and the Professor followed his lead.

"I go right past there if you want a lift," Joe offered.

"No, thank you. I want to stay on here for a bit."

They shook hands, and Joe said, "Thank you for your help. It's been nice meeting you. I am sorry we had to meet in these circumstances. We will keep you informed, and I hope your niece recovers soon."

He thanked Joe warmly and the Sergeant left the room.

On the way out he had a word with the WPC and looked at her notebook. Then he made his way home.

In the morning Joe reported his meeting to the DI over coffee in his office.

"You know, Joe, I've been going over Mel's report again, and there's no mention of them finding traces of semen anywhere in the house. Look – I am sure he would have carried on until he came; so there he is, wearing this rubber full of grunge, so what does he do? He takes it off. Now, you know as well as me that it's nearly impossible to get them off without some spillage or dribbling."

"But he could have waited until he was outside the house, boss."

"No, I don't think so. He wouldn't have risked it falling off down his leg. No, I reckon as soon as he got up off the bed he would have wanted to get rid of it."

"He could have flushed it down the loo."

"I don't think so, Joe. He would have wanted to get out of there as soon as possible, and you know it can be difficult to flush them

– especially the packet. No, I reckon he took it with him and disposed of it somewhere else."

Mid-morning saw the return of Mike and Jenkins. No, they hadn't had any luck. There was nothing to be found in the gardens or bins, and nobody was admitting to finding a condom. In fact, some of the people they asked didn't know what they were talking about – or so they said. However, word soon got round the nick, and by lunchtime a well-drawn cartoon had appeared on the noticeboard in the canteen, showing a picture of Mike with a condom on his head. The caption read, 'Has anybody seen my condom?' That brought some laughs. Even Mike took it in good humour.

After lunch I told Mike to pull a few bodies in – anyone local with a history of sex assaults. "Give them a roasting and see if you can come up with anything."

I asked Joe to follow me into my office and close the door. I told him what I had asked Mike to do. "That might convince the Chief we are doing something. Now, Joe, I am convinced it was someone she knew, so I want you to get a list of all the men she had contact with and run their names through the computer. See if you can come up with a suspect. Don't leave out anyone – milkman, butcher, postman, any repairmen. Check with the council – see if they have been doing any roadworks. Someone might have knocked on her door for a kettle of water. Check with the GPO. See if her telephone has been repaired lately."

"OK, boss, I'll get on to it straight away."

Joe got up and left. I sat back in my chair and clasped my hands behind my head. I was getting worried. We were getting nowhere. I could see the Chief calling in some help before long; then bang would go my chance of getting the credit. 'Why doesn't that damn woman wake up!'

CHAPTER 4

The phone rang, and my hopes rose when the switchboard told me it was the WPC at the hospital. She came on the line and I listened to what she had to say. Then, flinging the phone back on its rest, I rose quickly and hurried out into the main office.

"Forget what you are doing, Joe. That was the hospital."

"She's come round, boss?"

"No, I don't think so. The WPC says there's a row going on between the Doctor and the Professor. I think we had better get down there."

On the way I asked Joe what he thought about the Professor.

We were soon in the Doctor's room, and Joe introduced me to a very flushed-looking doctor and a very calm professor. Formalities out of the way, I asked the Doctor what was going on.

"You'd better ask him," he said with some anger, pointing to the Professor, who looked as if it was nothing to do with him. The Doctor carried on: "He wants to do some kind of experiment on his niece."

I turned to look at the Professor and into his deep blue eyes. He held my look for a couple of minutes then looked away.

I turned back to the Doctor and asked if there was somewhere we could speak in private with the Professor.

"Oh, you can use my office. I've got rounds to do," he replied, and he flapped out of the room.

I pulled a chair out and motioned for Joe and the Professor to do the same. When we were all seated I looked at the Professor again.

"So, Professor, what's it all about?" I asked, folding my arms.

The Professor looked at both of us then down at his hands, as if he was trying to make up his mind about something. Then he suddenly sat up straight and looked straight at me.

"Would it be possible to talk with you in private?" he asked.

"Look, Professor – anything you say about this case can be said in front of Joe."

"Yes, I do understand that, and I didn't mean any disrespect to the Sergeant in any way, but I would like to get your views on what I've to say first. You may think it's nonsense – if that is the case, then there's no harm done, just a conversation between two people – but if I speak in front of the Sergeant, then I believe you will have to file a report, put it on record."

"Yes, you are right, Professor."

I sat and looked him straight in the eyes for a few minutes, looking for a sign – of what I didn't know. None the wiser, I broke off the eye contact, looked at Joe, and asked him if he could organise some tea. He looked at me and said he would, but I couldn't read anything from his face regarding what he thought of the situation.

I watched him get up and waited till the door closed behind him before turning to the Professor, shrugging my shoulders and saying, "OK, the ball's in your court."

He looked at me for a second. "Now, what I have to say you might find hard to believe, but please hear me out before making a judgement."

I nodded.

"My research – well, I think it could be used to help you catch this man."

I sat up straight. "And just how could it do that?" I asked.

"Look, Inspector – what I tell you must be in confidence. You must not repeat it to anyone."

"Well, I don't know if I can agree to that if it's evidence."

"No, it's not evidence; it's more of a way of obtaining evidence. Look at it this way: if I could get you a picture of the man, would you need to know how I got it?"

"For Christ's sake, Professor! Are you saying you know who did it?"

"No, of course not – well, not yet, but I think I could get you a picture."

"This getting a picture, it wouldn't be illegal by any chance?" I asked.

"No, I can promise it wouldn't be illegal – highly controversial maybe, but certainly not illegal."

"So why the need for secrecy?"

"Because if news got out, then it could compromise my life's work and jeopardise my research. Therefore before I can help you I need your guarantees that you will not reveal my methods. What I am saying is that if I can give you the man's identity, then you will have to find other evidence to convict him. Anyway, I don't think anyone would believe you and I am not sure evidence obtained in this way would be admissible in court." The Professor folded his arms and sat back in his chair, as if to say, "I've had my say; now it's up to you."

I sat and looked at him for a while; then I said, "Look, Professor – before I agree to anything I will have to know more. There's a lot of people after my blood, and it would give them a lot of satisfaction to see me make a cock-up."

It was now my turn to fold my arms and sit back. We sat there staring at each other, then the Professor unfolded his arms and relaxed his posture.

"OK, Inspector, I think I can trust you. I will give you a brief outline of my research; then I will tell you how I think it can help. For the last five years I have been researching the brain – especially the part of the brain relating to memory. Now, when man designed the computer he was trying not only to duplicate the human brain but also to improve on it. Man wanted to have two brains – one inside his head and one outside. Now, what would the advantage of that be? Well, if your computer were a copy of the cleverest brain in the world, then you might think that the person with the stupidest brain could benefit from using this computer; but it doesn't work like that, because the computer can only do what it is told to do. The stupid person wouldn't know what to ask or tell the computer. So I've been working on connecting the brain straight into a computer."

"How does that benefit the stupid brain?" I asked to show he hadn't left me behind.

"Speed, Inspector. The keyboard is the biggest obstacle to human advancement in technology – it slows down; it obstructs through boredom. The human brain can process data faster than most computers, but the mechanical part of the human body stops the brain from reaching its full potential. Just think – if we could plug ourselves into a computer when we go to bed, in a couple of weeks we could probably put into our brains all the data that would normally take a lifetime to accumulate." He looked at me, daring me to absorb all he had told me so far. Finding I had no questions he continued: "I've been working with chimpanzees. Their brain is very similar to our own, and I am at the stage where I can actually retrieve data from and add data to the chimp's brain."

"You mean you can actually talk directly to the animal's brain, even though the animal can't talk!" I tried not to sound too sceptical, but he didn't seem to notice.

"'Talk', Inspector, is probably not the right word; 'communicate' is a better word. You see, the brain works on electrical impulses, and – guess what, if you didn't already know? – so does a computer, and there lies the secret of my success. I have developed software that enables a computer to analyse the brain's electrical impulses so we can understand them. Not only that, but it can convert new data which I put into the computer into impulses that the brain can understand."

"Jesus Christ!" I exclaimed. "And you can do all this already?"

He nodded with a smile.

"Oh, wait a minute, Professor – you said you have been working with animals. Have you – have you tried it out on humans yet?"

"No, but I can't see there would be any problems. I have compared the brain patterns of humans and chimps and can see no difficulties."

"So how does this help us with Miss Wood?" I asked.

"You remember I told you I had been working on the memory?"

I nodded.

"Well, I have read the report on how Susan was attacked and I think it's fairly certain she would have seen her attacker. If she did, then his face has been stored away in her memory for ever. Even if Susan can't recall it, it would be there."

"Professor, why wouldn't she be able to recall it if, as you say, it's there for ever?"

"The brain is a very complex organ. It is very protective and it tends to store unpleasant things away from direct access. Victims of assaults often can't remember being attacked; drivers often can't remember what happened just before a crash. It's usually put down as a mental blackout, but I believe it's the brain's way of protecting itself from something unpleasant. Imagine the memory section of the brain being like the shelves in a shop. Nice memories are stored on the shelves near to you; nasty memories are stored on the top shelves out of your reach, but they are still there. Another similarity between the brain and its counterpart the computer: if you input into your computer the fingerprints of a suspect, the computer searches through the data in its memory for a match; your brain works in the same way. Sometimes you see a face, but you can't put a name to it; then some time later it suddenly comes to you. Well, from the first sighting of the face your brain has been working, sorting through your memory data to match the face to a name."

'Christ!' I thought. 'This man makes so much sense it's frightening.'

"Now, if Susan were to suddenly wake up, it's possible she wouldn't want to remember such a traumatic event; there's no guarantee you would get the information you require, although we believe it exists somewhere in her memory. By using my method we could gain direct access to the information."

"You mean even now – while she's still in a coma?"

"Yes – especially while she is in a coma."

"Why exactly do you say that, Professor? Couldn't you obtain the information if she was awake?"

"Yes, of course. The state of the body is immaterial, but she might not consent to the – operation."

I sat there thinking for a minute.

"Professor, are you saying that, as her next of kin, you would give permission for the operation – experiment – even though you know she might not give that permission if she were awake?"

He nodded slowly.

"Look, Professor – you have got me worried. You are either very sure of yourself or a complete nutter. I am not convinced by what you've told me so far – not convinced at all."

"Very well, Inspector, I will try to convince you."

Why did I get the impression that he was actually enjoying watching me struggle to come to terms with what he was telling me? I somehow knew what he had told me was right, but I was having trouble admitting it to myself.

"Now, Inspector, as I have already said, the computer is a product of man. Man used his brain to produce a machine which can increase mankind's capabilities; that machine works in basically the same way as the brain. The main difference between the brain and a computer is accessibility. A brain can hold far more data than most computers, but we can't always access it. When we program a computer, it can takes days, months, years. Why? Because we are limited by the mechanics of the human body. When we see how fast a computer can process a complex calculation we are amazed, but our brain could probably work at the same speed if it wasn't restricted by our body. Now, when a computer produces a picture on its screen, it does so by arranging thousands of dots. Each one of those dots has its own electrical pulse, which identifies its shade, or colour; then the computer uses its memory to position it in the correct place on the screen. The computer has a data store – memory – just as the brain has."

"That's all very interesting, Professor, but how does that help us in this situation?"

"I am coming to that. Be patient. The software I have produced is a vast data store, which enables the computer to identify shapes, colours and sounds from their electrical pulse. Somewhere in Susan's brain is stored a set of pulses which, if accessed, would form a picture of the man that attacked her. Now, if she wakes up, she may be able to access the information and give you a description; but if the brain has buried the data, she may not immediately be able to remember. Later, when the trauma of the event has decreased, she may recall it, but that could take years.

On the other hand, Inspector, I could possibility give you that information in a matter of days." He sat back in his chair and folded his arms, which was his way of saying, "Over to you."

I looked at him for a while.

"OK, Professor, I am in no doubt that you could do what you say, but I have two questions. Firstly, how do you make the connection to the computer? Secondly, how, when you have established the connection, do you locate the correct data? I mean, I am sure I've read somewhere that the brain stores a person's entire life and—"

The Professor held up his hand to stop me carrying on. "Let me answer your questions. The connection is made using a thin needle probe. The probe is hollow and filled with miniature transducers. It is pushed through the skull into the brain."

He must have seen the way I cringed as he said that.

"Don't look so worried, Inspector. The brain doesn't feel any pain. You are quite right – the brain is very complex, but we only need to work in a very small part of it, and locating the correct data is not as difficult as you might think. During my research I found a definite difference between traumatic and calm memories. Here – I can show you best with a diagram." He took a notebook from an inside pocket of his jacket and opened it at a blank page. He found a pen in another pocket. "If we show an event in the shape of a wave, a calm event shows up in the memory as a nice gentle wave across the page, like this." He drew a gentle wave across the page. "A traumatic event would be, in contrast, like this." He drew a series of lines straight up and down across the page. The two are as different as classical music and rock music, and the computer can be programmed to recognise the differences."

I interrupted him with a question which had suddenly come to me: "What if there is more than one traumatic area? How will you know which one to access?"

I sat back in my chair, arms folded, and thought, 'Get out of that one!'

He sat looking at me for a while.

'Got him!' I thought.

"That is a very relevant point, Inspector, and I must admit it is one that baffled me for a long time, but then I discovered quite by accident that a traumatic event which had just happened has a longer time span."

"Time span?" I echoed. "What's that mean?"

"Well, the conclusion I drew is that the brain takes longer to process data relating to a traumatic event than data relating to a calm event. For example, we find it harder to remember a calm event in our lives than a traumatic one. A child is more likely to have a nightmare about a monster than a dream about an angel, don't you think?"

"Yes, Professor, I get the point."

He again sat back, arms folded, and he looked at me as if to say, "Next question!"

I shifted in my seat, feeling a little reluctant to ask my next question for fear of being made to feel small again.

"What about Dr Moore? Why is he so worried? He must feel there is a risk of some sort."

'Get out of that!' I thought.

"Inspector, if I wasn't 100 per cent sure there is no risk, do you think I would be talking to you now? I know we have only used animals so far, but I also know it will work on humans as well. Dr Moore's objections are based on ignorance. I can assure you that in the hundreds of connections we have made there have never been any problems – not even a minor infection. Now answer me this: do you think that Dr Moore could give you the same guarantee about his work? Do you think he could guarantee that Susan will ever wake up or, if she did, that she would be able to help you?"

He yet again sat back in his chair, arms folded. I was getting a bit tired of these dramatics of his. It's a wonder he never said, "I rest my case." I looked him straight in the eyes, looking for a sign of weakness.

'Make him look away first,' I thought. 'Show him who's boss.'

But I lost again. Those blue eyes stared back at me. I felt he was looking through my eyes into my brain, and I was the one who blinked and looked away to protect my sanity.

'What the hell!' I thought. 'What do I have to lose?'

"How long would it take to set up?" I asked without looking at him.

"Just a couple of days. I would need my equipment to be sent down. It's not very bulky."

"Is there any help you want from me?"

"Yes – I need a room and a measure of security. I myself will arrange everything with the hospital regarding Susan."

'Good!' I thought. 'I don't want to be too involved, just in case it all goes wrong.' As far as I was concerned it was between the Professor and his niece.

I got up to go and shook his hand. "I'll keep in touch." Just as I was opening the door, I turned back to him: "Professor, one thing: if Susan wakes up before you're ready, you stop until she says what she wants – OK?"

"Yes, of course, Inspector."

I found Joe standing outside talking to the WPC.

"Ready?" I asked him.

"Yes, boss. You all finished?"

I nodded.

We left the hospital and drove back to the office in silence. I know he must have been dying to ask what happened, but his professionalism told him that if I wanted him to know I would tell him in my own time.

CHAPTER 5

There was no sign of Mike or Jenkins; I asked Joe if he could find out what they were up to.

The next couple of days were filled with routine inquiries, and we interviewed the milkman, postman and any of Susan's other male acquaintances we could get our hands on. I pushed the team as hard as I could, hoping for that breakthrough we desperately needed. The pile of brown folders was growing higher on my desk, and the gloom I was feeling at the lack of progress was increasing, yet I knew the attacker's name could be sitting on my desk right at that minute; it could be in one of the folders. I stared at the pile, willing one of them to pop out and say, "Here I am."

I decided to pop in to see how the Professor was getting on. I found him in a small room, sitting in front of a computer. I looked around at the few items of equipment he had and I wasn't impressed.

"Is this it, then?" I asked sarcastically.

He looked up at me, but didn't say anything. He turned back to his work.

"Any progress?" I asked, trying to sound interested.

"Eh? No, not yet." His voice lacked the confidence of our previous meeting.

"Problems?" I asked.

"Well, yes and no. I've got the data from Susan, but I am having to alter the program more than I expected."

"How is Susan?" I asked.

"Oh, fine. Even Dr Moore's happy with her."

"So how much more time will this alteration take?" I asked.

"About another day, I would say."

He carried on tapping away at the keyboard, and I stood there for a while, staring at the back of his head, trying to transmit my thoughts into his brain. Finding that boring, I turned and left.

In the car on the way to the office I started to get a sinking feeling that everything was going wrong. I had now lost a lot of confidence in the Professor. I mean, if his program wasn't working properly, how did he know if he had the right data from Susan's brain? I could see it now: the Chief would call in some young graduate from the yard and he would spot the little clue we had overlooked and solve the case with his Filofax; and I would end up being transferred to school crossing duty.

Back at the office my feeling of despair was compounded as I watched the rest of the team just going through the motions. I knew they were waiting, expecting me to come up with some masterstroke. After all, I had told them I was the one with the knowledge, hadn't I? I knew there must be something we had missed – some stupidly obvious clue. It was probably staring us in the face, camouflaged by apparent insignificance, but I was sure it was there – such clues always were. I felt sure we would find it, but by then it might be too late – for me anyway.

The next morning saw me in front of the Chief with a glowing progress report and the promise of an early arrest. I sent the others out to make yet more inquiries, while I returned to the hospital more in desperation than in hope.

The Professor was sitting in exactly the same place as when I had left him the previous day. He looked up as I entered. I noticed that his face seemed more relaxed – dare I say, more hopeful.

"How's it going?" I asked.

"Fine. I've done the program and I'm almost ready to start the conversion process."

"Really?" I said with a renewed interest.

"Yes. I found two sets of data which indicate a traumatic event."

"Two sets?" I repeated. "Does that mean you will have to process both of them?"

The feeling of gloom returned as I thought two sets would take twice as long.

"No. I've selected the one with the longest time span as that must be the most recent."

"You don't think they might be connected?" I asked.

The Professor stopped typing for a minute as if in thought.

"No, I am fairly sure they're not connected."

"Wouldn't it be safer to process both sets?" I asked.

"We could do, but it would take longer, of course, and I will need another computer."

"Why is that?" I asked.

"Well, the amount of data involved is too big to store on a floppy disk, so I have to work entirely on the internal hard drive. That's just big enough for one set of data and the program, and I don't want to wipe it clean to make room for the second set of data – not before I've completed my investigation."

"Oh, I see," I said. I didn't really, but what the hell!

I asked if he would like a coffee, and left him to it while I went in search of one of those machines that every hospital has, according to the TV and films, except this one. But I did find my favourite WPC, who, in return for my best smile, offered to make a couple of coffees for us in the nurses' room.

I had a nice little chat with her while I waited; then, taking the coffees, I returned to the Professor. I sat on the spare desk in the corner and watched him at work. Words would stream across the screen and he would tap furiously away at the keyboard.

'Who is controlling whom?' I thought.

My thoughts were suddenly interrupted by the Professor: "I think it's coming together." Despite the calm way he said it, I could detect a tremor of excitement in his voice.

I stood up and walked over and stood behind him, where I could see the screen. The lines of words and numbers suddenly disappeared and the screen went completely blank.

"What's happened? Is it broke?" I asked in panic.

"No, it will take a few minutes for the picture to appear," replied the Professor.

"What sort of picture will it be?" I asked as I watched the screen anxiously.

'Surely it shouldn't take this long!' I thought to myself, although the Professor didn't seem concerned.

"It won't be a full action replay – just a still photograph if we are lucky. I have been toying with the idea of feeding the data on to a video tape; then we could play the whole memory like a film, but I am afraid that won't be possible for some time yet."

I was concentrating so hard on the screen that the sudden appearance of white dots in a line across the top of the screen startled me.

"Is that it?" I asked, sounding as disappointed as I felt.

"No, of course not. Be patient, Inspector. The computer is working very hard. It will compose the picture line by line."

Just then two more lines suddenly appeared; then the lines started to appear more quickly until they reached the bottom of the screen.

"That doesn't help much," I said.

The picture on the screen showed the outline of a face, but it was like a negative and not very clear. Not for the first time, the Professor ignored my sarcasm and just carried on tapping away at the keys. Tapping one with a final flourish, he swung round in his chair, looked up at me and watched the horror on my face as the picture dissolved off the screen.

"You've lost the picture!" I wailed.

"Really, Inspector, you should learn to have more confidence. It's not gone; I've transferred it into an art program which, I hope, will enhance it so we can see it better. All right?"

"Yes," I said with a grin. "You had me worried there for a minute. Look – something is happening."

He swung back to the screen, which had just changed from black to white. As we both stared, an outline started to appear as if someone was using an invisible felt tip. By the time it reached the mouth, I was staring in disbelief.

"The two-faced bastard!" I exclaimed loudly, causing the Professor to look up at me.

"You recognise him?"

"Oh, yes," I replied, not taking my eyes off the now completed picture on the screen. "Oh, yes, I know him all right. Well done, Professor," I said as I patted him on the shoulder. "Can you do me a copy of that?" I asked.

"Yes – no problem."

He tapped a few keys and the printer suddenly chattered into life. I walked over to it and watched as that face appeared dot by dot. Cruel anger was clearly visible on the face, as if it were twisted by some physical exertion. As soon as the picture was complete I ripped the paper out of the printer and stared at it for a few minutes; then I carefully folded the paper and put it in my inside pocket. Suddenly realising the Professor was watching me, I looked at him rather sheepishly and felt rather humble.

I patted the pocket I had put the paper in and said, "Thanks, Professor. Thanks for everything. I am sorry . . . Well, you know." I shrugged my shoulders.

I think he knew that I was trying my best to apologise for questioning his ability, but I think he was probably used to dealing with doubters.

"That's all right, Inspector. I understand. However, don't forget our agreement – no one must know."

I nodded and left the room.

The journey back to the nick flew by, not because of my speed but because I was deep in thought. The way I swaggered through the office caused the team to look up in anticipation, but I kept a blank face. I looked at Joe and motioned with my eyes for him to follow me.

In my office I dropped into my chair. Joe pushed hard to close the door, then turned to face me and waited. I picked up the pile of folders and threw them to one side.

"We missed him, Joe. He is not in there."

Joe looked puzzled. "You mean you know who it is, boss?"

I nodded, enjoying the moment.

I took the folded picture from my pocket and passed it over. I sat and watched his face as he unfolded the paper. I saw his face darken and his eyebrows rise as he realised whom it was a picture of. He looked at me with bewilderment.

"Can't be, boss. It can't be."

I smiled. "Oh, yes, it can, Joe. There's no doubt about it."

He looked down at the picture again and shook his head. Looking at me again, "Where did you get this from?" he asked.

"Straight from the horse's mouth – straight from the one person who would know."

"Oh, you mean the Wood woman. She has woken up, then?"

"No, Joe, she has not woken up – not as far as I know – but it did come from her."

"Then how did she give you a picture?"

"I am sorry, Joe – I can't tell you that; and I want your promise never to tell anybody about that picture. You see, we can't use it for evidence, so it doesn't exist – OK?"

He took a deep breath. "OK, boss," he said as he handed the picture back. He suddenly smiled. "The uncle, right?"

I looked at him and held my hands apart and shrugged my shoulders.

"So what next?" Joe asked, sitting down.

"We don't have a file on him?"

"Well, no, boss – we never put him in the frame."

"That's right, Joe. None of us suspected him; yet, when you think about it, he is the only one who could have done it. He is the only one she would have trusted enough to let in late at night. She would have never looked at him as a lusting male – it just wouldn't have occurred to her."

"Yes, you are right, boss. It all starts to slot in."

"That's right, Joe. He is the missing first piece – the key. So, Joe, I want you to handle this – start investigating him. We can't use the picture, so we need other evidence – but, Joe, keep it to yourself. Remember he has friends in high places. Keep Mike and Jenkins working on other leads and don't leave the file round the office. OK, now I think you should start by looking into his background. Check how long he has been in this job, previous employment, etc., etc. And, Joe, I don't want his boss getting wind of our investigation. I want it all sewn up before we go public – no loose ends."

"OK, boss, I've got the picture."

"No, you haven't; I have."

I picked up the picture off the desk and put it back in my pocket. We both smiled and Joe got up and left. I watched that damn door start its closing routine and grinned to myself as I thought about the can of worms I was about to open. Oh, yes, DI Watson was alive and well and on his way back. I would need to get the maximum publicity from solving this case. The Professor's need for anonymity was a bonus, as I could claim all the glory. Yes, sir, things were looking up. I would have to renew my acquaintances on the daily papers and call in a few favours that were owed; I might even get in touch with Sylvia and make up for lost time. Thinking about that brought back a few memories, and I smiled to myself as I sat there swinging from side to side with my hands clasped behind my head.

Later the next day I met Joe in a café on the far side of our manor. We found a quiet corner and he took the new file from his briefcase.

"So what have you got so far?" I asked him.

"I went through DVLA and found that before coming here he was at Adwell in Essex, so I found that they had a golf club. I noticed our suspect had a set of golf clubs when we were round there."

I nodded.

"I rang the club secretary and made out I was vetting him for a committee member. He knew our suspect very well. Not only that, but he didn't like him. Anyway, the rumour that went round was that there was a bit of bother regarding a lady."

I sat up. "What sort of bother?" I asked.

"It appears he got friendly with this woman – a spinster – and he rather misread the situation. But instead of accepting that she wasn't interested, he kept pestering her. She complained to his bosses, and when that didn't do the trick she made a complaint to the local police. As a result he was moved on to – well, we both know where to."

I carried on stirring my tea and waited while Joe sorted his notes.

"Here we are. I phoned Adwell nick, and the sergeant there remembers the case, but there is no paperwork. Apparently a deal was made that if he was moved, she would withdraw her complaint."

"This sounds promising, don't you think, Joe?"

"Yes, boss, and there's more: I checked back through some of the statements we have already got, and there was one from a woman opposite the Wood house who saw a man walking a dog that evening. Well, he has a dog and it matches the description of this one." He passed over a statement. "That's from a chap who lives in Jacks Road, opposite the park. He says he looked out of his window about seven thirty. Some kids were making a hell of a racket. He saw him in the park with his dog. He is certain it was him because he knows him. Now, if you look at this map" – he pointed to a red circle – "that's the Wood house, this is his house and this is the park. You can see that the only way to the park is right past her house. Now, consider this: on this side, in the opposite direction to the Wood house, is another park, which is half as far from his house as the one he was seen in."

"You know, Joe, from what you have shown me, I think he went to see Miss Wood that evening; when he found she wasn't in he carried on to the park; then, on his way back, by which time she would have arrived home from Mrs Thomas's, he called on her. No – hold on – he would have had the dog with him. No – he must have taken the dog back to the vicarage first, then gone round there. She let him in and bingo! It all seems to fit, but it's only circumstantial."

I sat there thinking and stirring my tea.

"You'll have a hole in the bottom in a minute."

"Eh? What? Sorry, Joe. You were saying – I was miles away?"

"Your cup – you will stir a hole in it."

"Oh, right."

I put the spoon in the saucer and took a drink from the cup.

'Yuk!' I thought. The tea tasted horrible, and I doubt whether it would have tasted much better if it was hot.

"Joe, this is what we will do: tomorrow the Chief's off all day, and the weekend too, on a course, so early in the morning we will go and pull him in. That'll give us plenty of time to break him down, get a confession and have the whole thing wrapped up by the time the Chief gets in on Monday. That way his boss can't get on to the Chief and pull any strings."

"Are you sure this is the best way, boss? What about if he didn't do it? I mean, the evidence we have so far wouldn't convict a drunk for jaywalking."

"I know, Joe – but he's guilty, I can feel it. Trust me. We'll nail the bastard to the cross if we have to. When you get back to the nick have another go at Adwell. See if you can get a statement from that woman he was messing about with. Then, tomorrow morning, I'll meet you at the office at six o'clock and we can go and lift him out of bed. That should shake him up."

"Six o'clock, boss – good grief, it's a bit early! It's all right for you: you don't have a grumbling wife. She hates being woken up at that time, I can tell you."

"Well, don't wake her."

"You are joking. If I sneak out without her knowing and checking I've got a clean shirt on, then, well, I wouldn't dare go home again."

I laughed at the pained expression on Joe's face. I could just picture his wife at that time of the morning, bell tent for a dressing gown, head immersed in curlers. She was a big lady was Betty and looked formidable at the best of times, let alone early in the morning.

'Well, Joe,' I thought, 'you are more than welcome. I don't envy you – not one little bit.'

CHAPTER 6

The next morning, at about six thirty, saw us banging on that large oak door. Only policemen, it seems, can knock in such a way that the occupants immediately know there are police at their door and they are in trouble. We usually have to bang a few times, which adds to the drama for the occupants – but not this time. The door was flung open quickly, just as Joe was about to deliver the follow-up knock, and he almost fell through into the hallway. The tall, imposing figure stood above us, not looking at all intimidated, but fully dressed and in command of himself.

"Yes, Inspector. What can I do for you?" came the stern inquiry.

Just for a few seconds I lost it. "Ah, yes, could we have a few words with you about the Miss Wood case?" I asked.

He looked at his watch. "You seem rather early."

Joe spoke: "We thought we might catch you before your day began."

"Um. You had better come in, then, but I can't spare you very much time. I've a lot to do."

We followed him into the same room as before, and he sat down behind his desk. I could feel that we were losing the initiative as we took our seats.

"Well, Inspector, how can I help you? I am sure I've told you everything."

"Ah, no, sir, I don't believe you have told us everything."

He looked at me, puzzled, worried. "I don't quite follow. What exactly do you mean?"

"Well, sir, it now appears that you called round to see Miss

Wood on the night she was attacked."

"How did you—?" He stopped.

"How did we know, sir? We have a witness."

The confidence melted away from his face and was replaced with a worried frown.

"Well, I might have; I am not really sure."

He leant back in his chair and stared up at the ceiling. I knew he was playing for time, trying to compose his thoughts.

I motioned to Joe, who said, "Reverend Thomas Wright," – the vicar's eyes shifted from the ceiling to Joe – "we would like you to come down to the station to make a statement."

Joe's voice sounded seriously official, and I could see the fear and sadness in the vicar's eyes as the words sunk in.

Joe stood up. "Are you ready, sir?" he asked, holding out his hand as if to help the vicar to his feet.

"What – now, you mean? Right at this minute? Impossible! I have things to do."

I now stood up and said, "Please, sir, will you come now?" I tried to sound as threatening as possible.

He turned to look up at me, his face sagged and white. He slowly got to his feet and followed Joe, with me bringing up the rear.

Out in the hall Joe stopped and asked if he wanted his jacket, pointing to the clothes hanging neatly from their brass hooks.

"Ah, yes, thank you," said the vicar as he reached out and took a grey jacket. I looked at the golf clubs standing proudly at the side of the hatstand as the vicar fussed about putting his jacket on. I could tell he was playing for time – thinking time.

He suddenly turned to Joe: "My dog I can't leave – he's in the kitchen."

"That's all right – I don't expect you will be long," I said. He seemed to perk up a bit when I said that.

Not a word was said as we drove back to the station. I sat in the back with the vicar, who stared out of the window all the way. He must have been deep in thought as he was startled when I told him we had arrived. He followed Joe meekly, shoulders sagging slightly, to the interview room. I closed the door with a controlled bang, which had the desired effect of making the vicar jump. After we had all sat, I pointed out to him that he was there of his own free will to help us with our inquiries and that he was free to leave at any time. He sat bolt upright, looking down at his hands, which were palms down on the table, as if he was about to get up. I felt he was showing us that he was ready to leave at any moment he chose.

I started the questions: "Now, when we saw you the first time you told us that the last time you saw Miss Wood was on the Monday afternoon when she was on her way to Mrs Thomas's. Is that correct?"

He nodded without looking up.

"But our subsequent investigations show that you did in fact see her on the evening she was attacked."

"No! That's not true. Yes, I did call to see her, but she wasn't in. I told you the truth before."

Still he did not look up. I noticed that he was now clenching and unclenching his fists as if in some sort of pain or turmoil.

I carried on: "After calling at Miss Wood's what did you do then?"

"Well, I had my dog with me so I carried on to the park, to give him a run."

"Which park did you go to?" I asked.

He looked at me, puzzled. "The one at the end of Miss Wood's road of course," he snapped.

"That's right," I said.

"Well, if you already knew, why did you ask?" His voice lacked the normal anger I am sure he would have shown under different circumstances.

"Why exactly did you call on Miss Wood?"

"I was worried she might forget about our appointment the following morning. The church magazine proof had to be at the printer's by nine thirty."

"Couldn't you have phoned her?" asked Joe.

"Yes, I could have, but I was going out anyway to take the dog for a walk."

"Did you go round to Miss Wood's often?" I asked.

52

"No, not often – just now and again. She was kind enough to invite me round for tea, and sometimes supper."

"So you have been round to Miss Wood's in the evening on other occasions, then?"

"Yes, Inspector, I have, but not on a regular basis." He tried to sound as bored as he could as he answered. "Is all this relevant?" he asked.

I ignored his question.

"When was the last time you went round in the evening?"

"Let me think." I could sense he was getting his confidence back. "That must have been a couple of weeks ago. I remember that because we spent the evening working on the magazine; it comes out fortnightly."

"Couldn't you have worked on the magazine at the vicarage?" asked Joe.

"We do usually, but we get too many interruptions. You should try to understand that being a vicar is a twenty-four-hour job. Anyway, Susan suggested we finish it off round her place."

I felt the vicar was starting to take over, so I fired another question at him: "What time did you leave the park?"

He looked at me in surprise, as the tone of my voice reminded him we weren't there for a cosy chat.

"Why, the light was just going – I would say about eight thirty."

"Which way did you go back?" I asked.

"The same way as I went, of course. There is no other way."

I nodded. "So you went back past Miss Wood's house, then?"

"Yes, it would be impossible to go any other way, unless you think I suddenly sprouted a pair of wings and flew back," he answered sarcastically.

"And the dog," Joe said.

The vicar gave him a dark look and said, "Quite so."

"Did you notice that Miss Wood was now at home?" I asked.

"Yes, I did. The lights were on."

"So you went and knocked on her door again?"

"No, of course not," he answered angrily, obviously thinking I was trying to trick him (as if I would!).

"Are you telling me that you went out on purpose to speak

with Miss Wood, but then changed your mind?" I asked in my best sarcastic voice.

"It was getting dark. She probably wouldn't have opened the door," replied the vicar, shifting in his chair.

"But you said you often went round in the evening, for supper," I asked with a doubtful look.

Again the vicar fidgeted in his chair. "Yes, yes, but then she would have been expecting me, wouldn't she?"

He was looking a bit edgy, so I asked him if he would like a cup of tea. He nodded and I looked at Joe and we got up and left the room. Out in the corridor I collared a passing PC and asked if he could rustle up some cups of tea.

"Well, Joe, what do you think?"

"I don't know, boss. I mean, we have got nothing – nothing that will stand up in court."

"I know, Joe, but he's the one, Joe. I can smell it. Take off the collar and he's just an ordinary man like you and me. He's got feelings, urges, and in his job he is surrounded by all these adoring women, like groupies round a pop star – temptation, Joe. And we know from Adwell that he can be tempted."

"You know, boss, I've never thought of the WI as being a load of groupies."

I laughed at the look on Joe's face as he spoke.

The PC came back with the teas and we returned to the room. The vicar's face was expressionless as I placed a cup in front of him. I think I detected a murmur of thanks. All seated again, we sipped at our drinks.

Then I asked, "Can you tell us why you left your former parish at Adwell?"

That shook him. He looked at me, then at Joe, then back at the table.

"That was years ago."

"But why did you leave?" I asked again, persistently.

"My bishop thought a move would be good for me."

"So it wasn't anything to do with one of the ladies – a spinster like Miss Wood – making accusations against you?"

"Look," he said sternly, "I was not forced to leave. It is quite normal for the Church to move vicars around. I was asked to come here to regenerate the parish."

"Are you saying that our records are wrong and that no complaints were made against you?" I asked, trying to make what I had said sound totally unbelievable.

He looked hard at me. "Inspector, I have just explained the reason for my move. I admit there was a rumour circulating that I had been paying too much attention to one of the ladies, but that was idle gossip, born out of jealousy – part of the hazard of being a vicar. I can assure you it is quite commonplace among the clergy."

"So you are saying there is no truth in the rumour, and the lady in question made it all up to discredit you."

"No, Inspector, I am not saying Miss Cook was lying – just that she misunderstood the reason why I helped her. Good grief, man! I've helped hundreds of people – it's part of my job. Look – I've had enough of this. I am a very busy man, so can you please arrange for me to be taken home?"

He started to get up, so we followed suit. I stood directly in front of him.

"In that case, Reverend Thomas Wright, I am arresting you for the assault and rape of Miss Susan Wood."

The vicar turned ten shades of white and sat down again, looking totally petrified. I carried on telling him his rights, but I don't think he heard a word. I turned to Joe and asked him to take the vicar through to the custody area. Joe moved round to the vicar's side and took hold of his arm. The vicar stood up in a total daze and Joe took him out of the room.

When Joe entered the custody area with the vicar, Sergeant Bert Sole was pinning a notice up. He turned and saw the vicar first, then looked at Joe.

"What have you got here, Joe," he asked, looking bemusedly at the vicar.

Joe explained the charge and he filled in the forms. He had to ask the vicar several times to confirm his name and to empty his pockets. The vicar was still in a daze. I don't believe he understood what was happening to him. Mind you, he woke up quickly enough when Bert asked him for the chain and cross round his neck. Bert solved the problem by lending the vicar a Bible in its place. Joe watched as he was led to the cells. He couldn't help feeling a bit sorry for him. Joe wasn't totally convinced that he was guilty, and he suspected that we wouldn't be able to hold him for long. Joe was glad I was in charge. There were some advantages in being just a sergeant at times like this. He made his way up to my office.

"Got him tucked up, Joe?"

"Yes, boss. Look – are you sure? I mean, we don't have a lot in the way of evidence."

"Joe, I know it's all circumstantial, but it all fits. Sit down. This is what I am sure happened: he did call on his way back from the park; she let him in as she had done many times before, only this time she was in her dressing gown, according to Forensic, having just got out of a bath. They went into the front room and sat down; then he saw a bit of bare leg or whatever. He got excited, got her upstairs and couldn't stop himself. That's why he came back the next day. He would have realised that she couldn't have phoned us or we would have been hammering on his door, so he thought there was a chance to throw himself on her mercy – beg for forgiveness and all that. He must have nearly died when he saw you were already there. That's why he was so irate with you and didn't give you his name. Did you notice, from the WPC's notebook at the hospital, that he has visited Miss Wood every day – not out of concern, I'll wager. He wants to be there in case she wakes up so he can convince her it was an act of God or something. It all fits, Joe."

"I know, boss, but what worries me is are we making it fit?"

I nodded. I could see Joe's point.

"Look, Joe – get a warrant and take Mike and Jenkins down to the vicarage. See what you can find. I don't think we will be allowed to search the church – not officially anyway."

"OK, boss. I'm on my way."

Joe knew I was probably right, but he would have felt a lot happier with some good solid evidence behind him.

They got back from the vicar's just after lunch. Joe never enjoyed going through people's lives. It made him realise how shallow life was and how little in the way of personal possessions most people actually have. He knocked and entered my office, and placed a labelled plastic bag on my desk. I looked hopefully at the bag.

"Find something?" I asked.

Joe pointed to the bag. "There are some cards and letters from females (nothing incriminating), two packets of condoms (one opened, two missing, one still sealed), a mail-order sex catalogue and a couple of girlie magazines. That's about it."

I looked at Joe. "Well, what did I tell you? What would an unmarried vicar want with condoms?"

"Search me, boss."

"Good work, Joe. Get this stuff over to Mel and ask her to work her magic. Tell her that if she gets an answer to me this afternoon, she can have me as a slave for a day."

"I don't think you would last a day – not with Mel, boss."

Joe grinned as he left and I smiled to myself. I was feeling quietly confident. A few minutes after Joe had left, Bert Sole rang me. He told me the vicar wanted to give his bishop a ring to arrange a relief for some of his duties. He was also worried about his dog. I told Bert to tell the vicar I would inform the Bishop. There was no way I was going to let him talk to the Bishop. I didn't want him pulling any strings. I asked Bert if he could arrange to have the vicar's dog collected and looked after. I asked the switchboard to get me Bishop Woodley. A few minutes later the phone rang and he was on the line. I was going to enjoy this – spoil my day off, would you!

"Sorry to bother you. DI Watson. I am in charge of the Miss Wood case. Yes, sir. I've just called to let you know that we have made an arrest and the suspect is in custody now."

I listened as he heaped on the praise – how wonderful the British police were, etc., etc.

"Oh, by the way, I have a message from the Reverend Thomas Wright. He asks if you could arrange for someone to stand in for him at his parish. Oh – didn't I say? – he is the one we have arrested in connection with the attack on Miss Wood. No, sir, I can assure you we haven't made a mistake." There was a few minutes' silence at the other end of the phone. "I am sorry, sir, but the Chief won't be back until sometime next week. Goodbye."

I put the phone down. Oh, boy, did I enjoy that! Revenge definitely is sweet. I sat there for a few minutes gloating in my glory; then I suddenly had a thought. I got up from my chair and went out into the main office. Good – Joe was there.

"Joe, where does the Bishop live?"

"He's got a big place out at Wemsly, boss."

"How long would it take him to get here?"

"Thirty to forty minutes, I should say."

I stood there thinking.

"Can you let Custody know we will want to interview the vicar in about twenty-five minutes?"

"OK, boss."

I went back to my office and sank down in my chair. I was feeling smug, to say the least. If the Bishop did turn up, as I thought he might, he wouldn't be able to see the vicar until we had finished our interview, which could take a long time. A masterstroke, eh!

When it was time for the interview, I collected Joe and we made our way downstairs. I filled Joe in on my thoughts regarding the Bishop, and Joe, being Joe, pointed out that the Bishop could turn up with a solicitor for the vicar and get to see him that way.

We collected the vicar and returned to the interview room. Joe loaded the tape machines and explained their use to the vicar. I reminded the vicar that he was still under caution and asked if he would like a solicitor present.

"No, Inspector. I have no need for a solicitor, because I am totally innocent of these preposterous allegations – a fact that will soon become crystal-clear, even to you, Inspector."

The vicar sat back in his chair, arms defiantly folded. I looked at him. The spell in the cell seemed not to have had the effect on him that I had been hoping for. He looked confident and composed.

"Let me assure you, sir, that the reason we are here is to establish the truth. Now, I want to go over the facts we have established so far so that they can be recorded. If we seem to be asking the same questions as before, please bear with us."

The vicar sat there, unmoved by my words.

"Now, you have told us that the last time you saw Miss Wood was on the afternoon of the 12th at about two o'clock. Is that correct?"

"Yes," the vicar answered abruptly.

"You also told us that later that same day at about 7 p.m. you called at her house."

"Yes, but she wasn't in." Again the vicar spoke abruptly.

"You then carried on to the park in Jacks Road and stayed there until after eight o'clock."

"Yes."

"You say you then returned home, walking past Miss Wood's house, but although you could see that she was in you did not call on her."

"Yes."

The vicar just sat there, displaying no emotion, as though he was conducting a funeral service. I hoped to God it wasn't mine.

"About what time did you arrive home?"

"I am not sure. Probably about a quarter to nine."

"So you passed Miss Wood's house at about eight thirty?"

"Yes, I suppose so."

"Did you notice anybody while you were walking?"

"No."

"When you got home, did anyone call on you or phone you?"

"No."

"What was the first thing you did when you got in?"

"What do you mean?"

"Well, did you turn the light on, put the cat out, phone somebody, check for messages . . . ?"

"No. The light was already on, the cat has a flap in the back door, and I didn't call anyone."

"You say the light was already on?"

"Yes."

"Do you always leave the light on when you go out?"

"No, of course not – only if it is dark."

"But when you went out it wasn't dark. You said you were in the park when it started to get dark."

"No – yes, that's right. Perhaps I was getting confused. Perhaps the light wasn't on." He looked a bit flustered and fidgeted in his seat.

Seeing he was losing his composure, I pressed home my advantage: "Could I suggest that you are not confused, and that when you saw Miss Wood was home you rushed home, putting on the light as you entered? You then left the dog and returned to Miss Wood's house, and she, trusting you as a friend, let you in, and you repaid her trust by attacking and raping her!"

"No! No! I didn't go out again. I stayed in. I keep telling you."

The vicar's face was crimson with the frustration and effort of trying to make us believe him. I allowed him time to calm down before I continued. I didn't want to have to explain a suspect dying of a heart attack while being questioned.

"Reverend, have you ever been married?"

"No, Inspector, I have not."

"Have you ever visited prostitutes for sexual reasons?"

The vicar went a bright shade of red. "Are you mad? How can you suggest such a thing! For God's sake, remember who I am."

"I know who you are. You are man, just the same as me and Joe, with the same natural urges."

"No, I am a vicar."

"That's just your job, like Joe and I are policemen, but first you are a man, with normal man desires. Your job means you are surrounded by all these unattached women, like Miss Wood. Is that what happened at Adwell with Miss Cook? Did the temptation get too much, the urges too strong?"

"No! I told you that was all a misunderstanding."

"I know what you told us, but we know the reality is something different, don't we?"

The vicar looked down at his hands as he fidgeted with them. I picked one of the plastic bags up from the floor where Joe had placed them and tossed it on to the desk in front of the vicar.

"Are these yours?" I asked. "For the tape, I am showing the Reverend Wright a bag containing two magazines of naked women and a mail-order catalogue for sex aids."

The vicar's face went back to condition red. "You've been to my house. It's an outrage. You've no right – no right at all."

"We have every right. We are investigating a very serious crime; and, I might add, if Miss Wood should die, then it will become a murder inquiry!"

The vicar's face changed from the red of anger to the white of fear.

"Now, are these yours?"

"Yes – I mean no. I found them."

"You found them? Exactly where did you find them?"

"In the church – in the choir's changing room."

"So why did you keep them? Why didn't you destroy them? Why did you keep them in the drawer in your bedroom?"

"I was going to destroy them, but I forgot."

"Now, you have stated that you are not at present having any sort of sexual relations. Is that correct?"

"Yes."

"Well, Reverend, can you explain these?"

I reached down and picked up the other bag and dumped it in front of the vicar on top of the first bag.

"For the tape, I am showing the Reverend Wright a bag containing two packets of condoms. One packet is complete and unopened; the other packet is opened and two of the three condoms are missing."

I sat and watched the vicar – clearly a man having a crisis with himself. He was staring down at his lap, his shoulders visibly sagging. He looked a beaten man – a wreck of the person we first brought in. "Well, Reverend, I am still waiting for you to explain why we should have found these condoms in the same drawer as the magazines in your bedroom!"

Still the vicar didn't reply.

"Do you understand the question?" I asked.

"Yes," the vicar answered softly.

"Can you speak up, please, for the tape?"

The vicar, still looking down, said, "Yes," louder this time.

"So can you answer the question?"

"No."

"Are you saying that you are refusing to answer the question?"

"Yes."

I sat back in my chair and looked at the vicar sitting there, head bowed.

I glanced sideways at Joe, who took my hint and said, "Do you realise, sir, that if you refuse to answer the question we must draw our own conclusion?"

The vicar looked up from his lap, first at Joe and then at me. "Inspector, I couldn't care a damn what conclusion you wish to fabricate, because the truth of the matter is that I'm innocent, and as far as I am concerned that is the end of the matter. I refuse to say anything else." With that, the vicar sat upright and folded his arms.

I looked hard at him but he avoided any eye contact, so I instructed Joe to terminate the interview and return the vicar to the cells.

Joe took the vicar and I sat there thinking until Joe came back.

"Were you guessing about the dog, boss?"

"Yes, Joe, but, if you remember, Forensic found no dog hairs anywhere, so I reckon when he saw she was in he rushed home to get rid of the dog (he wouldn't want the dog leaping around and barking) and, most importantly, a condom. He wouldn't want to put her in the club – there's no way he could cover that up. Perhaps he thought he was on a promise. He might have misread the signs, as I am sure he did in Adwell. Who knows? Anyway, there's a special sitting at the magistrate's court in the morning. Get him remanded into our custody – no bail, interfering with witnesses, own protection, the usual."

"Right, boss, I'll sort the paperwork."

We both went back upstairs. I struggled to close the damn door; then I picked up the phone and made a call.

"Hi, Sam. Roger Watson. Long time since we spoke."

Sam was a reporter I had known for a long time. We helped each other from time to time.

"Look, Sam – we are putting a body up in court tomorrow morning. Yes, I know it's Saturday. It's for the Susan Wood rape. Yes, that's right. Guess who, Sam? It's the local vicar. Yes, I thought that might interest you. Reverend Thomas Wright. That's right –

charged him myself this morning. No, we are going for remand in custody and no bail. And, Sam, I never told you – OK? You owe me."

I made a couple more calls to other reporters I knew. There's nothing like a bit of publicity and reporters in court to shake the bastards up a bit! By the time I left for home the Bishop still hadn't arrived. I must say I was disappointed, but then again he probably wanted to make sure he didn't catch any of the mud when it started to fly.

The next morning I was sitting in my office when Joe got back from court.

"How did it go?" I asked as he came into my office.

"Fine. We got a remand till Wednesday. Oh, and by the way, when we got there the place was crawling with press. The vicar wouldn't get out of the car until I put my coat over his head. You wouldn't have had anything to do with that, would you, boss?"

"Who, me, Joe? No, of course not. I expect the press bung one of the court clerks to tip them off if anything juicy comes in."

"Well, I can tell you the vicar wasn't very pleased."

"Well, that is a bloody shame – don't you think so, Joe?" I looked at my watch: twelve thirty. "Joe, I want to have another go at him before we knock off. Perhaps the court experience has made him see sense."

"I wouldn't bet on it, boss. He was pretty mad when we banged him up."

Thirty minutes later the three of us were back in the interview room, the vicar sitting there in his defiant mode: bolt upright, arms folded across his chest. I went over the previous day's questions again, but with no response. I tried a few new questions, but failed to get an answer.

Finally I said, "Reverend, I don't think you are helping yourself with this attitude."

"Helping myself! I came here – no, was tricked into coming here – and I have been treated like a common criminal, locked up in a filthy cell, paraded in court for everybody to see, chased by reporters – and God knows what lies they will be printing! – and you say I am not helping myself. You're mad – crazy. The world's gone mad. I am innocent, *innocent.*" The vicar's eyes wildly blazed hatred at me.

"Well, sir, the evidence we have seems to prove otherwise. As you know, you have been remanded into our custody until Wednesday; then you will appear in court again, only this time it will be a committal hearing. That means you will be committed for trial at a Crown Court, so I strongly advise you to treat this matter seriously. I also advise you to contact a solicitor." I paused to let what I had said sink in. "Now, is there anything else you wish to tell us?"

The vicar sat there, unmoved and silent.

I terminated the interview and Joe took him back to his cell.

We returned briefly to my office, and then we left to enjoy what was left of our weekend.

On Monday I presented myself and the evidence we had to the Chief. I sat quietly as he read my report.

"Well, Roger, a turn-up for the book! Who would have thought it would be the vicar!" He passed the file back. "That" – he pointed to the file I was holding – "is a bit light, Roger. I think you will need more to feel safe."

"Yes, sir, I agree. We are hoping for a statement from the Adwell woman, and, now we know who it was, I am expecting other evidence to surface. We should be all right by the time we get to trial – and there's always a chance that the Wood woman will wake up."

"I hope so, Roger, because I feel that with a member of the clergy involved this case will attract a lot of attention."

'I hope so,' I thought.

"So make sure it's watertight. By the way, how is Miss Wood?"

"Still no change, sir."

The meeting over, I left. Once I was back in my office, I breathed a sigh of relief. I had expected to find the Bishop with the Chief, or to find out he had been on the phone breathing fire. Perhaps his staying away was a sign that he believed, or knew, the vicar was guilty. Perhaps he had confessed to him.

I called Joe in and told him what the Chief had said, and asked him if he had any news from Adwell. He told me that Miss Cook was away at present, but should be back by Friday.

During the lunchtime I popped out to the local paper shop. On my return to the office I dumped the papers I had bought on Joe's desk.

"Make sure the vicar gets these, Joe."

Joe picked up the top paper and read the headline. He whistled through his teeth.

"You don't believe in mercy, do you, boss?"

"No, Joe, not with people like him. There could be loads of women out there who have been messed about by the likes of him and are probably too afraid of what he represents to complain. Not only that, but bishops cover things up to protect the good name of the Church. In any other job such people would be thrown to the vultures, as I know from personal experience. With a bit of luck, when the Reverend Thomas reads these reports he might see how hopeless things are and do the decent thing and give us a confession. Mercy, Joe? Nothing doing!"

After the Wednesday hearing, the vicar was committed to trial, owing more to a friendly magistrate than to our evidence. The vicar was remanded to our cells because of the prison officers' dispute. They were refusing to accept any more prisoners until their grievances were met. That suited us as we wouldn't have to travel every time we wanted to interview the vicar. There still was no sign of the Bishop, but a solicitor had turned up to help the vicar, and I was sure he had been sent by the Bishop. They could communicate through him and we would never know. The trial date had been set for five weeks' time, so I thought I would take a long weekend off to make up for my previous time off being interrupted.

CHAPTER 7

On the Friday, I packed a bag and went off on a whim. I had always wanted to visit Wales, so I just drove there. I drove around until I found a nice-looking bed and breakfast, 'found' being the operative word as I was totally confused and lost by the time I turned into the gate. I parked in front of a delightful stone cottage which had been toned by time and the weather. The sign at the gate looked neglected and forgotten, but my anxious knock was answered by a woman drying her hands on her apron. She was – well, of ample proportions, to say the least, but she had a very pretty face; I suppose she was in her mid-forties. By the enthusiastic way she greeted me, I guessed she wasn't overrun by visitors. Yes, she had a bed and I was most welcome.

The room she took me to was a gem: cosy, with a low ceiling and a huge iron bed. The window was low down so I had to bend down to glimpse the view across the valley. The descending dark was already kissing the tops of the hills. I was grateful when she offered an evening meal, as I hadn't passed any cafés or pubs or anything resembling civilisation on my way and I was starving. I had a wash in the quaint little bathroom, and laid on (well, laid *in*) the bed. The mattress was about three foot thick, and so soft. The darkness spread through the room, searching every nook and cranny for any remnants of daylight.

I must have dozed off, as I was dragged abruptly back into the land of the living by the alien sound of a gong echoing through my brain.

It took me a few minutes to realise where I was; then I rubbed my face and struggled to get up from the bed, the softness absorbing my arm as I tried to find some leverage. Finally I rolled off and landed on my knees and hands on the floor. I stayed their for a few minutes as my fingers felt the texture of the home-made rug, then I got to my feet, my eyes now accustomed to the half-dark. I made my way to the door and out on to the landing. I was grateful that the light which leaked from the heavily shaded bulb was a mellow yellow, instead of the usual eyeball-searing white glare.

I made my way down the narrow stairs and followed my nose into an old-fashioned kitchen. The well-scrubbed heavy table was set with two places. My landlady, Gwen, appeared through a door to my right.

"Please sit down, Mr Watson. Make yourself at home," she said in a lovely, kind voice, which you would have sworn belonged to a nice young blonde had you heard it on the phone.

I took my place at the table and spent the next hour and a half enjoying the best meal and company I had ever had. After the meal we sat in front of a real fire and I completely forgot my past as I entered a fantasy world devoid of problems and worries as I listened to Gwen talking about her simple life and expectations. The smoky air played havoc with my unaccustomed eyes and I was soon feeling tired. I made my excuses and went up to my bedroom.

The cool, refreshing air in the bedroom reversed my tiredness. I drew the curtains and selected a paperback from the little shelf and sat in the old armchair. As soon as I started to read the tiredness returned and I must have nodded off.

I woke with a start as my elbow slipped off the chair arm, and I looked round the room, puzzled, until I realised where I was. I looked at my watch: I had only been asleep for a short while. I stood up and stretched away the stiffness, and I decided I would go to the bathroom. I collected my toilet bag and towel from my still-packed suitcase and made my way along to the bathroom. I was just about to open the door when a voice started to sing softly from the other side of the closed door. I quietly cursed my luck, and was about to turn away when I noticed the light poking out through a slit in the aged wood. I stood on my toes and I strained to peer in.

My eyes widened as I saw the rear view of Gwen – a naked Gwen – as she leant over the bath to turn off the taps. The width of her bottom took my breath away. The hairy mass of flesh of her private parts was clearly visible as it was squeezed backwards by the expanding flesh of her thighs. I gasped in wonder as she half turned as she swirled the water with her hand. Her breasts hung straight down and were at least a foot long, and I watched mesmerised as, free of all restrictions, they swung gently in time with her movements. The magic of the moment was broken as, with a sigh, she stood up and heaved her bulk into the bath. Only her back was visible, and I licked my dry lips as the disappointment released the tension that had locked my body. I pulled my eye away from the door and sank back down on to my feet, feeling for the first time the pain in my tortured toes. A wave of guilt flooded over me – not because of my peeping, but because I realised that in the excitement I had been rubbing my knob. Looking down, I took my hand away from the hardness that was tenting my trousers.

I walked painfully back to my room and closed the door. I leant back against the door. My hand brushed my hardness and I was engulfed by a feeling of pleasure. I closed my eyes and remembered what I had seen. I imagined coming up behind Gwen as she leant over the bath, and caressing that width of flesh, reaching underneath and feeling that hairy mound, parting those heavy lips and feeling the sticky warmth, then guiding my throbbing shiny knob up into her and hearing the smack as my body thrust against her soft buttocks, reaching down to steady her swinging breasts as I jerked into her, feeling her hand as she reached back and caressed my swinging balls, and the sudden ecstasy as I came and collapsed across that broad back.

'Bloody hell!' I said to myself as I realised that in all the excitement I had rubbed myself off and could feel the wetness in my underwear.

I cursed as I took my trousers and underpants off. I used the pants to dry myself. Not having brought a dressing gown, I put my trousers back on and pulled the zip up carefully.

Taking up my book again, I settled down to wait for Gwen to finish in the bathroom.

The next couple of days I spent walking the local area. Despite my spying, I was not able to catch Gwen in the bathroom again, and during my journey home I wondered if she would have obliged had I asked. After all, Gwen with her clothes on was, I expect, a turn-off for most men, me included, so I don't expect she had many offers. I spent a good part of the journey fantasising about bonking Gwen, always from the rear. Just think of getting all that flesh moving on a waterbed! My thoughts were terminated by the stark reality of being home back in the rat race, a fact highlighted by the pile of junk mail on the mat. I bet Gwen never got any – I don't imagine she was on anyone's mailing list.

The first thing I noticed as I entered the office first thing on Monday morning was that Joe wasn't at his desk. Joe was almost always first in, almost always at his desk when I arrived.

'Perhaps he is in the loo,' I thought.

I checked my watch: eight forty-five. Well, I wasn't *that* early. I settled down in my chair to wait.

'Come to think of it, there is no one in the outer office either – no Mike or Jenkins. Perhaps there is a flap on.'

I reached out to pick up the phone to see if I could find out where everyone was. Suddenly the phone rang, making me jump.

I grabbed the handset and said my name. It was the Chief – could I go straight up? His tone didn't sound too friendly.

I bounded up the two flights of stairs and nodded to the Chief's secretary and tapped smartly on his door. I entered in reply to his instruction. Joe and Mike were already there, sitting in the two spare chairs, which meant I would have to stand. I nodded to Joe and Mike, noting their obvious embarrassment. I turned back to the Chief and waited for him to explain what was wrong; I didn't have to be a brilliant DI to work out all was not well.

The Chief spoke: "Reverend Thomas Wright—"

"Not topped himself, has he?" I butted in.

The look on the Chief's face told me that wasn't the cleverest remark I could have made.

The Chief continued: "We have been working on this case all weekend."

I glanced a puzzled look sideways at Joe, who fidgeted nervously in his chair.

"Why?" I asked. "Have there been some new developments?"

"That, Inspector, is quite an understatement." The Chief spoke with a new sternness in his voice. "The Wood woman came out of her coma on Saturday morning."

"Well, that's good news. Will she be all right for the trial?" I asked.

"Roger, there won't be any trial."

"You are joking," I said. "You don't mean she is not going to press charges."

The Chief held his hand up to instruct me to be quiet. "The reason there won't be a trial is because it wasn't the Reverend Wright."

"Of course it was. The evidence!" I blurted out angrily. I looked at Joe for help, but he was busy counting the daisies on the carpet.

"No, it wasn't the Reverend. The Wood woman has made a statement. I was there. Joe will give you a copy, and you will see that she clearly states that she didn't know her attacker, who was wearing a mask. You will also notice that the description she gives in no way matches the Reverend Wright. She describes the man as short and fat and having a gold tooth."

I felt dazed. My mind flashed back to the picture on the screen. What had the Professor said?

"Two areas!" I mumbled out loud.

"What did you say?" asked the Chief.

"Oh, nothing," I replied.

'The Professor must have picked the wrong data,' I thought.

"Roger, Roger," – the Chief brought me back from my thoughts – "we have to sort this mess out quickly. I've released the Reverend into the Bishop's charge while the paperwork is finalised, and I have released a press statement. I want you to go over to the Bishop's and explain to the Reverend that all charges made against him have been withdrawn, and to apologise for our incompetence."

"Apologise!" I echoed. "But it was him – I know it was."

"No, Roger, it was not the Reverend. I told you your evidence was flimsy; you should have waited."

"It was him – I know it was."

The Chief ignored my whingeing.

"I suggest you get on. I have some calls to make to try to sort out this damn mess." The Chief's voice quivered with anger as he spoke.

I turned on my heels and stormed out. Joe and Mike jumped to their feet and hurried after me. I reached my office in record time and slumped down in my chair. Joe tapped on the door nervously and came in. He pushed hard on the door for a few minutes before turning to face me.

"I am sorry, boss. We tried to find you. . . ."

"Joe, you know as well as I that he did it – he was the one – so what the hell happened?"

"Well, it was just after dinner time on Saturday. The Chief called me at home. He said he was at the hospital and he wanted me to meet him there at ten o'clock on Sunday morning to take a statement from the Wood woman as she had come out of her coma."

"So you have seen her?"

"Yes, boss. On Sunday morning I met the Chief and took her statement."

"How did she seem?"

"All right. She was clear and positive – seemed to know exactly what she was doing."

"She must be protecting him, Joe. She must be."

Joe shrugged his shoulders as if to say he was just doing as he was told.

"Didn't you question what she put in her statement? I mean, her description doesn't match with the forensic evidence – surely you noticed that!"

"Yes, boss, I did, but the Chief just wanted me to take the statement; he gave me no chance to ask any questions."

"OK, Joe. Thanks. I want you to come with me to the Bishop's. I'll call you when I am ready."

Joe left my office.

I sat there thinking for a while. There was something wrong – I could smell it. I picked up the phone and asked the switchboard to get me the hospital. After a delay they managed to locate Dr Moore for me. I asked him how Miss Wood was. He told me she was doing fine – almost back to normal.

"It must have been quite a shock, her suddenly coming round like that," I said.

"Yes, totally unexpected. I rang the Bishop straight away."

"You rang the Bishop? Why?" I asked.

"Well, as she has no immediate family the Bishop left specific instructions that he was to be informed the minute she came round."

"What about her uncle?" I asked.

"Well, he had returned home to take his equipment back, so we couldn't locate him."

"But you did try?" I asked.

There was a long silence at the other end.

"So what happened then?" I asked.

"Well, he came rushing in and asked to see her alone. Having spent about an hour with her, he asked to use my phone. About thirty minutes later another man arrived. They spent some time talking in my office, then they both went in to see Miss Wood. Then they both left. The man, whom I hadn't seen before, informed me that he will be back in the morning to take a statement from Miss Wood."

"The Chief and the Bishop! Well, what do you know!" I thanked the Doctor and rang off.

I swung round in my chair, hands clasped behind my head. Now I knew: the Bishop must have put the fear of God into her. He probably told her what she had to say; then, when they had got their story straight, he called the Chief, and the Chief was duped into collaborating with the story. End of case! But the Bishop and Miss Wood don't know about the forensic evidence, so they just made up a description – which was exactly the opposite to the vicar's, just to make sure, beyond any doubt, that we can't proceed against him. It was funny, but I didn't feel angry any more. I knew he was guilty; Miss Wood knew; the vicar and the Bishop knew; and God Almighty certainly knew. And they all knew that I knew; and that I knew would give them a few sleepless nights, wondering if they were safe, knowing I would be watching, waiting for that mistake.

Feeling better, I collected Joe and we made our way to the Bishop's residence. We were shown into an enormous sitting room, so big it had three sets of settees and chairs as well as tables, bookcases and enough pottery to start a shop. We stood waiting, watching the door.

It seemed ages before we saw the handle turn and in walked the vicar. He looked completely different from the broken man I had left in the cells.

"Good morning, Reverend," I said in a voice which sounded so normal it surprised me.

"Morning, Inspector, Sergeant," he replied. "Do sit down." He was certainly beaming with confidence.

We declined his offer.

"We have come about the Miss Wood case. I've been instructed to inform you that all charges made against you regarding the case have been withdrawn."

"All the charges, Inspector?"

"Yes, sir – all the charges."

"What a surprise, Inspector! Isn't it a pity you didn't believe me when I said I was innocent? Instead you twisted the truth to suit yourself, fabricating lies. You destroyed me. I've lost my church, my credibility; all the good work I've done – gone! Do you really think it is that easy? You have violated my life, and you will pay – pay dearly, Inspector."

I motioned to Joe and we made to leave. I didn't want to get into a slanging match as the Bishop was probably listening outside the door – the Chief as well, I shouldn't wonder. Joe went through the door first.

"Oh, Inspector."

I turned back to face the vicar.

"I've got a present for you."

He passed me a small paper bag. I looked at it with suspicion. 'Is it something nasty?' I thought.

I opened it and looked inside: a condom. I looked at the vicar.

"You never know, Inspector, it could save your life one day."

"Just one thing, Reverend – one thing we both know as well as a couple of other people – and that is you are guilty. You did it."

The Reverend Wright's eyes narrowed with hate.

"And another thing: He knows too." I looked upwards as I said that.

He followed my glance and blushed.

I turned and left. I followed Joe out through the front door. I felt the rush of air on my neck as the door was slammed behind me.

Back at the office, I went through the files again and again, but, like the Chief said, there was not a lot in the way of concrete evidence. I thought of interviewing Miss Wood. Perhaps if I showed her the picture her uncle had obtained, told her where it had come from . . . But what if the shock sent her back into a coma? What if she complained to the Bishop? What if . . . ? What if . . . ? Oh, my God, damn the bloody Church! Whatever the Bishop had said to her had had such an effect that she had lied to the police, of that I was sure, so her fear of the Bishop was greater than the moral issue of lying. Or perhaps she didn't look on it as lying – more a way of protecting the Church, being a martyr. I threw the files into the out tray in disgust.

Two weeks later I received a letter from the Chief: I was being lent to another force as part of an inter-force exchange scheme. I was ordered to report to the Chief Super at Wheyton, a small town north of Tolchester. A quick check on the map told me what I had feared: I was going to be a long way from the Met – a bloody long way. More punishment! And how come my new appointment started in just five days' time? I knew that the force never usually moved that quickly. You would normally be given at least three months' notice of such a move. And why didn't the letter say how long the move would be for?

My thoughts were interrupted by a knock at the door, and Joe came in. He had heard about my news on the grapevine and was sympathetic.

"Don't worry, boss – you will soon be back."

"No, Joe, I don't think so. More likely they will send me off on another scheme after this one, and another after that. You know, Joe, not a year ago I was at the top, with a lifestyle to match; now look at me. In a few days I'll be as far from the Met as you can get."

Joe nodded. "But at least you will still have your rank, boss."

"Oh, yes, I mustn't forget my pension," I replied in a sarcastic tone. I looked up at Joe. "Sorry, Joe – I shouldn't take it out on you."

"That's OK, boss."

He turned and left me to my misery, and thoughts: 'I wonder what the women will be like up there. Probably all prim and proper, no sex before marriage, have you got good prospects? Ah, some hope! Then again, it could be wild country. I might have to get used to being dragged into haystacks or barns by burly farmers' daughters to satisfy their primitive desires and lusts.'

CHAPTER 8

Wheyton was worse than I had feared – a small, decaying farming town, which had become a dormitory for the nearby city of Tolchester. They hadn't had a murder (not even a suspicious death) for years. There were plenty of petty crimes, but, unlike Milton, there didn't even seem the chance of anything more serious happening. Oh, I mustn't forget the rustling! It had never occurred to me that people went round nicking sheep or cows – well, not in this country. 'Perhaps I had better learn how to ride a horse and throw a lasso,' I thought.

My new colleagues were a good bunch, though a bit basic about life. The major topic of conversation wasn't women, but fishing. As you can imagine, I felt out of it at first. It was like listening to a foreign language.

I rented a nice detached bungalow – very nice. The garage had an electric door, so I didn't have to get wet if it was raining.

I had been there for a couple of weeks, and was finding it quite pleasant and relaxing. In Milton, there had been much more pressure. If you went to the loo in Milton, you tended to hurry, whereas here the loo seemed to be a meeting place. There always seemed to be two or three people having a debate there about some new rod or reel. Everything seemed to be done at half speed, but, despite this, work was done. Even the radio transmissions seemed relaxed. An outsider listening in would have thought he was listening to some local radio station dedicated to fishing. The controllers in the Met would have gone mad. When I asked the desk sergeant (whose nickname, by the way, was Pike) if the Chief Super ever complained, I was introduced to the cunning side of rural policing.

"No, lad. When he first came in he was a bit of a problem. He didn't like the idea of us carrying our tackle in the pandas or the way they always smelt of fish, so we introduced him to the president of our club, Lord Simms. The Chief Super, being a bit of a snob, was impressed – even more so when we voted him on the committee as vice president. He's been as good as gold ever since."

At first I found it difficult to fit in, despite the fact I was treated so well. The difficulty was of my own making. Firstly, I was carrying round a grudge at being sent here; and secondly, how could I take a job seriously when for the life of me I couldn't see what possible benefit my gaining experience of rural policing would have on my career in the Met – unless, that is, I wasn't expected to return, and this was the beginning of the end. But I found, despite all my reservations, that after a few weeks I was beginning to enjoy myself, my life, in a way I never had before. I think it was all down to working with people who were completely down to earth and honest – honest about themselves. They all worked for one another; there was no back-stabbing or trying to score points off one another. In short, they were a complete team, fishing for crime! If they got a good result, it was referred to as 'a good catch', and never '*I* had a good catch', but always *we*. The same applied if a mistake was made by anybody. *He* didn't get the blame directly; *we* accepted the responsibility.

Even Joe Public was different. It had never occurred to me that there were actually people in the world that couldn't read or write, or didn't have a bank account or credit card, but there were. Not only that, but they seemed to survive very well. It was completely new to me the way people seemed so willing to help one another rather than themselves, more willing to give than to receive. I must say, as I went out amongst these people I was very suspicious of them at first. I mean, they actually seemed happy with what they had, which in some cases wasn't a lot. I could see the contrast between their contented attitude and the way my parents had slaved away to buy a bigger and posher house and car – they always seemed to be working for something. I can never remember hearing my parents laugh together, never remember seeing them with their arms round each other. They simply never had time for each other. I now met people who didn't even lock their front doors; they had nothing worth stealing, so they didn't have to live out their lives behind locked doors, jealously guarding their possessions. They just enjoyed life.

I began to realise that the way most of us live is stupid. We fight our way to the top of the pile, through fair means or foul, then spend the rest of our lives fighting off people who want to take our place. It is the same with possessions: we buy expensive things, then spend our time worried that someone will steal them from us. Rather than giving ourselves more and more things to worry about, we should learn to enjoy ourselves instead. Yes, my outlook on life was changing for the better. I even went fishing with Pike a couple of times and caught some fish. And – you know what? – I felt more satisfaction than nabbing a bank robber red-handed.

At about this time I got a letter – well, a note – from Joe: 'Hi, boss. I hope you have settled in well. Just thought you might be interested in the enclosed.'

I unfolded the newspaper cutting and saw a wedding photo. The happy couple beamed up at me, causing me to frown. I read the caption under the picture: 'Miss Susan Wood, of this parish, was married today to the Reverend Thomas Wright. The Bishop of Milton officiated.' The only thing missing was the Chief as best man. I stared at the smiling Miss Wood, and I realised that I had never seen her with her eyes open before.

'Well, Susan, was that your price for keeping quiet?' I wondered.

I carefully folded the cutting and note and put them in the drawer of my desk. I sat and thought back over the Wood case. It made me realise how the Met had become nothing more than a political weapon. Results won votes, won promotion. No wonder there were so many innocent convictions and so much corruption! It wasn't about people any more – the stakes were too high. Everyone was fighting one another to get to the top as fast as they could. Blow the people! Blow law and order! I wonder if those back in the Met realise what a big favour they did me. Being at Wheyton might not improve my policing skills, but it certainly improved my outlook on life and my quality of life. Little did I realise that events were about to unfold which would change my life for ever.

Pike came to see me and gave me a memo headed 'ARP'.

"What's ARP?" I asked.

"Animal rights protesters," he replied. "It's that time of the year again."

I looked at him, puzzled.

"Hunting season. As soon as the hunts start up they come out from under their stones."

"Trouble?" I asked as I studied the memo.

"Can be. If it's just the locals, then no trouble; but if some of the professional mob turn up from the city, then it's big trouble. It used to be a nice day out, but then the city louts appeared, organised and violent. You'll need to swot up on this."

Pike passed me a thick folder, and I flipped through the pages, noting that some of the pages had coloured photos.

"I keep it up to date. They're the bad lot – the ones with a red line. They're the nasties. They go from place to place just stirring up trouble. Tom Busby, the chap who took your place in London – well, one of them broke his arm last season, hit him with a three-inch post when he wasn't looking. Mind you, we are lucky just having the two hunts; Tolchester's got four or five, and they have to cover the research lab. That's been done over a couple of times that I can remember. Still, it serves them right. I don't like animals being used that way myself."

"What exactly do they do there?" I asked.

"I don't rightly know. I've only been there once. It gives me the creeps. They have lines of cages, mainly monkeys, just sitting there zombie-like – vacant eyes, no sign of life, not natural. I am glad we don't have to deal with the place."

I looked up at Pike. "Where exactly is the lab? I might pop in and take a look if I am passing sometime."

Pike looked at me for a second, then gave me directions. I made a mental note to take a look the next time I was over at Tolchester.

A couple of weeks later I was on the way back from an interesting lecture on drugs at HQ at Tolchester when I found myself subconsciously taking the long route, which according to Pike would take me past the research lab. I soon spotted the car park he had told me about and pulled in. I parked facing the heavy chain-link fence. The area behind the fence looked like a park. There was no sign of any movement; the place look deserted. I could see some buildings semi-concealed by a screen of trees and bushes.

I got out and followed the concrete path round to a small metal gate adjacent to the large, heavy main gates. The gate squealed as I pushed it open.

Pushing open a white wooden door I entered the gatehouse. An aged security guard faced me across a worn counter. I would have been impressed by his alertness, but he must have been warned of my approach by the squeal from the gate.

"Yes, sir, can I help you?"

"I've come to see Professor Edward Mark."

"Is he expecting you, sir?"

So he did work here! I had known it would be a long shot.

"No, not exactly; but if you tell him DI Roger Watson from London is here, I am sure he will see me." I flashed my warrant card.

"Yes, sir. Please take a seat and I will try to locate him."

I sat down on one of the plastic chairs surrounding a small table sprinkled with a few magazines. The wall opposite was covered with some posters which looked like they had been purloined from a travel agent's. I heard the mumble of the guard's voice on the phone.

'I wonder what the Professor's reaction will be,' I thought. 'I expect he knows what happened – probably went to his niece's wedding.'

Five or ten minutes must have passed before the door off to my left suddenly opened and a man in a white coat came in. It was not the Professor.

"Mr Watson," he said, holding out his hand.

I stood up and shook hands.

"Tim Brown, Professor Mark's assistant. I'll take you over."

I followed him out and we made idle conversation as we walked towards the buildings I had seen behind the trees. As we neared the complex I could see the buildings were all single-storey, and in the centre was a fairly new red-brick structure. All the other buildings belonged to an earlier era – a wartime military camp or something similar. I was impressed by the overall tidiness of the place. We made our way up the clean path to a glass door in the new building.

Tim pushed open the door and I followed him into a small hall. There was only one other door and that was to the right. Tim opened this door and we entered a small room. I could see from the furniture, which was almost identical to that of the gatehouse, that this too was a waiting room.

Tim gestured to a chair. "If you would care to wait here, the Professor will be with you shortly. Would you like tea, or coffee?"

"Coffee, please," I replied.

I sat down as Tim left the room through a door which I noticed was fitted with a security lock. I strained to hear any noise, but the place was totally silent. A few moments later I turned as the door opened and in walked the little man with the very blue eyes. I stood up quickly.

"Mr Watson," he said as he approached me, his face beaming a smile, "how nice to see you again."

We shook hands like long-lost brothers.

"Please – please sit down," he said.

I sat down in my seat and he sat in the chair facing.

"I hope you don't mind me dropping in like this."

"No, not at all. Are you still with the police?"

"Yes, I am – locally actually."

"Locally?" the Professor echoed, looking a little puzzled.

"Yes, I am based at Wheyton – part of an inter-force programme," I explained.

"Oh, I see. I did wonder what happened to you. I thought I might have seen you when I came down to Susan's wedding."

"No, I was already up here. How is your niece, by the way?"

"Oh, she's fine, but I am still puzzled by her choice."

We exchanged a few more pleasantries, and then he asked, "Are you here officially?"

"No, I just thought while I was up here I would look you up."

The Professor looked a little relieved at my answer.

"Well, it is nice to see you, Roger; and thank you for not saying anything about our project."

"Did you tell Susan?" I asked him.

"No, I realised you hadn't disclosed anything, and Dr Moore was keen not to bring the matter up, so I thought it best not to. Anyway, she wouldn't have understood."

"No, I suppose not."

The anger I had felt towards the Professor had all evaporated some time ago, and it had been replaced by a yearning to know what had gone wrong.

"Tell me, Professor: what do you make of all this? Do you think we got the wrong man?"

The Professor thought for a while.

"Well, it's possible. We no doubt got the right data, of that I am sure; however, it's possible that Susan was so emotionally involved with the vicar that her mind substituted his face for that of the attacker. You see, she might have wanted it to be him who made love to her – so much so that her mind took over her memory. In many ways my experience with Susan has added new dimensions to my research, and I believe we recently confirmed what I've just said."

"New dimensions to what?" I asked.

The Professor looked at me, studying my face. Then he leant forward in his seat. "You know, Roger, from the first time I met you I felt I could trust you. I could tell that your interest in my work was professional, rather than for personal gain."

"Yes, I must admit I am fascinated by what you are doing, but I am worried as well. You are delving into the unknown; however, the benefits to the human race could be enormous."

"Quite so, Roger. Now let me explain what I have been working on lately – strictly in confidence, mind you."

I nodded. "Of course – you have my word."

I looked at him with renewed interest. I was keen to hear what he had to say.

"Good, good. I think you will find I have moved on from what we did with Susan." His eyes were sparkling with excitement. "Now, if you think back to what we did with Susan, we extracted data from within her brain and analysed it so we could make sense of it."

I nodded.

"Well, that made me think: the fact that we could decipher information stored in the brain suggested that we might also be able to produce information in a form that the brain can understand, and transmit that information directly to the brain."

The Professor had lowered his voice as he spoke, and I automatically did the same: "What would the advantage be in doing that?" I asked in a hushed voice.

"Well, just think for a moment. When we are born our brains are almost empty; then as we progress through life we accumulate what we call knowledge. The amount of knowledge is related to the amount of time we spend learning, which again is related to the amount of time we are awake. Given that the average person sleeps for half their life, we could say that we lose fifty per cent of our learning time. In fact, it is much higher than that. There are times when we are awake when we don't actually learn anything. For example, a person working on an assembly line learns at first, but then they do the job automatically. They don't learn any more. They spend their time daydreaming."

"So what you are saying, Professor, is that you could add knowledge to a person's brain while they are asleep."

"That's right, Roger. Just imagine: you could have almost twice as much knowledge than you have now."

"Yes, I can see that would be an advantage to someone in my position, but surely that wouldn't apply to everyone. I mean, there are some people you just wouldn't want to be brainier – the common criminal for one."

"You're right, Roger. That's why the system would have to be properly controlled. In the wrong hands it could be more devastating to the human race than a nuclear war. That's why there will have to be a controlling body. I am convinced that the future world will need exceptional people to both control it and protect it. Back in the Second World War the Germans were already working towards achieving a super-race for that purpose, but they concentrated on producing the perfect physical specimen. I want to produce the perfect brain."

"Wow, Professor! It sounds as though you want to take over the world."

"No, no, Roger, that's not what I want. I want to help save it, before mindless, crazy, greedy people destroy it!"

The Professor was visibly angry at my suggestion. I fidgeted uneasily in my chair as I realised I had upset him.

"I am sorry—" I started to say, but he interrupted.

"That's all right Roger. Your reaction is certainly understandable." He had quickly regained his composure.

A knock came at the door and Tim came in with a tray, which he put on the table. I welcomed this break, as I am sure the Professor did. It was an interlude to enable us to recompose ourselves. I felt the conversation had been heading down a one-way street. We both picked up our cups and settled back in our seats. We sipped our drinks while we studied each other. I wondered what he was thinking. Almost together we replaced our empty cups on the tray, the rattle of the china (none of your sterile plastic here) breaking the nervous silence.

The Professor took the floor again: "Anyway, back to what I was saying: my research has progressed to the stage where I have had some success in adding information to a chimp's brain, and in doing so I have been able to exert a certain amount of control over the animal's behaviour."

"Do you mean you can control the animal as you would a robot?" I asked, trying to mask the concern I was feeling.

He ignored my question and carried on: "Take the common criminal: you know from personal experience that no matter how often he is caught and punished he will still offend."

I nodded.

"And at present the best we can do is to explain that it is because he came from a broken family or had a mixed-up childhood."

Again I nodded. I remembered the hundreds of times I had been pounded with these excuses by the do-gooders who appear as if by magic every time a criminal is arrested. The more appalling the crime, the stronger the excuses are.

"Roger, I will tell you that person has a fault within his brain. It was there from the day he was born, and it will be with him the day he dies. No amount of locking-up or therapy will cure him. Oh, I know some people go straight after being locked up, but that doesn't mean they have been cured; it just means their fear of being locked up is greater than their will to offend. Now, what if we address the problem directly – replace the faulty data with correct data? We could change this criminal into a responsible person."

"Do you think that will be possible?" I asked. I could see my job becoming redundant.

The Professor's eyes were sparkling again. "Yes, of course, Roger. Why wait for a person to offend to find out if a person has criminal tendencies? Why not test children at birth? It may even be possible to correct other brain abnormalities and to reverse brain damage."

"Professor, I notice you use the word 'correct' and not 'control'."

The Professor smiled. "I believe people would accept being corrected or cured, but if they thought you were trying to control them – well, you can imagine the outcry."

I sat looking at him, trying to weigh him up. Was he a complete nutcase or a genius? Was this the future I was looking at? Were humans destined to be controlled like robots by a chosen few? If it was decided that you weren't a satisfactory person, would you be corrected?

"Tell me, Professor: why me? Why are you telling me all this? Why not tell the world?"

He looked at me with a serious expression. "Roger, what I've told you is completely confidential. No one else knows – not even Tim. I certainly can't tell the world – not yet – not until my work is completed and safe from ridicule." The Professor paused. "As for telling you, Roger, I know I can trust you (you showed me that over that business with Susan) and I can see you are interested in my work, and I may need your help shortly." Before I could ask another question, he added, "That's all I can say at present."

I didn't push the point; I decided to try a different path: "Tell me, Professor: just how much control do you hope to achieve over the brain?"

"Well, Roger, it's early days yet, but, as an example, we had a young chimp delivered and I got Tim to torment it by repeatedly taking its food away – nothing physical. After a while that chimp really hated Tim – so much so that he used to go wild every time he came into the room. Then I added some correcting data to the chimp's brain. The next time Tim went in the chimp welcomed him like a long-lost brother. It really shook Tim up, I can tell you."

"Tim didn't know what you had done?" I asked.

"Good God, no! Tim's a great assistant, but he hasn't the intelligence to understand what I am doing."

"Is that why you chose him?"

The Professor looked at me as if he was impressed by my intelligence. "Yes, I once had a very clever assistant who ran off with all my notes on another project. They made quite a name for him." I could see the hurt in his eyes as he spoke. He suddenly slapped his knees. "Ah, well, that's all in the past now."

He stood up, and I followed.

"I am sorry – I have to go. Unfinished work." We shook hands and he half turned to leave, then stopped. "Roger, I've enjoyed our chat. Would you be interested in helping me?"

"Yes, I would, but I would need to know more details," I replied.

"Yes – quite so." The Professor stood there deep in thought. "Look, Roger – I need to think. Can I get in touch with you when I am ready?"

I took out one of my cards and wrote on the back. I passed the card over to the Professor. "That's my home number," I told him. "If I am not there, you can call the office and leave a message."

The Professor put the card in his pocket, smiled and left. A few minutes later Tim came into the room and took me back to the gatehouse.

On my way home, I reflected back to my meeting. I couldn't believe I had offered to help – help with what, and why me? Was it because he trusted me, or was it because of my job? What if it were illegal? No, I decided, I would only help if there were no comebacks. I couldn't afford any more setbacks to my career – uh, what career?

CHAPTER 9

It must have been three weeks after my visit when the Professor phoned, and I agreed to meet him for a drink. I followed his directions to a small pub, well off the beaten track. I found him already there, sitting in a corner. Apart from us the place was empty. I sat in the seat opposite him.

"Lager all right?" he asked, pointing to the glasses on the table.

"Yes, fine," I replied.

I noticed that the glasses were just halves. It was a long time since I had held a half-pint glass. We spoke about the weather and other trivialities for a few minutes, then he put his glass down and stared at it for a few moments. I put my glass down and sat waiting. He suddenly looked up and fixed me with a stern look.

"Roger, what are your thoughts on what you know already?"

'Um,' I thought, 'it looks as though I am being tested.'

"Well, I found what you said interesting, and naturally I am curious to know how I can help. I wasn't frightened by what you said, but I did feel threatened. I suppose that is because I don't like the idea of being controlled or interfered with. I do realise that your work could be of enormous benefit to the human race, but (and it's a big but) in the wrong hands, used in the wrong way, it could be disastrous. You know, after our last meeting I had a dream. I was in this large room with hundreds of other men, and we had to sit on a conveyer belt and go through a tunnel filled with blinding flashing lights. When we came out the other side, we all looked the same and spoke with the same voice, and we had to go through a door which said 'POLICEMEN'." I picked up my glass and took a drink. Putting it down, I said, "And I don't think that's as far-fetched as it sounds, is it?"

"No, probably not, Roger, but what is the alternative? A world ruled by force, by war. How long before nuclear weapons are available to anybody who has the money? How many more people need to die in the name of peace? How many nuclear explosions does it need to destroy the world? Given the choice, wouldn't you opt for control?"

"Yes, but how much control? I mean, are you saying why build robots when you can turn people into robots?"

"Well, Roger, I think it will come to just that one day, but not in our lifetime."

We sat in silence for a while, sipping our drinks. Why did I like the man? Perhaps he made more sense than anyone else I had met. Perhaps subconsciously I could imagine my bosses in the Met thinking I was the best copper in the world. Why shouldn't I be the boss? Why stop there? Why not prime minister? The fantasy drifted through my mind. I could have the most beautiful women in the world – as many as I wanted – ready to satisfy my every whim and desire.

"Roger, Roger." I was brought back to reality by the Professor. "Roger, are you all right?"

"Yes, yes, I am fine," I replied. "I was just thinking, Professor. You said you wanted my help."

"Yes, I need your help to move on to the next step."

"Which is?" I asked.

He hesitated, looked at me, then leaned closer to me. I automatically mimicked his movement.

He spoke quietly and calmly: "I've gone as far as I can on animals. I need a human – a human brain."

I jerked back in my seat so suddenly that I startled him. I looked at him.

"You mean me?" I asked angrily, folding my arms defensively.

"No, no, of course not." His voiced sounded alarmed and he looked at me anxiously.

I stared back defiantly and said in a stern, monotone voice, "I think you had better explain."

"Look, Roger – I thought we could find somebody, a down-

and-out, tramp, someone who has no connections, no family – someone who would be willing to help with my research. In return I could pay him, look after him." He was almost pleading.

"What about the risk? What about if you scrambled his brain so much he ended up as a vegetable, or even dead?"

"Roger, I would never proceed with my work unless I was sure. Do you think I would have used Susan if I wasn't sure? Do you think I am some sort of monster?"

"No, Professor, I know you are not a monster, but I can understand what your research means to you, and I can understand that you might overlook the risks when you are thinking about the results."

"Yes, I see your concern, Roger, but I can assure you that I have considered all the points you have made. I have thought about the risks. To be honest, I cannot completely guarantee that nothing will ever go wrong; but, then again, nor can you."

I sat up at this accusation. "What exactly do you mean by 'nor can you'?"

"Well, Roger, you are a policeman, a custodian of an area, of people in that area. Can you guarantee that every one of those people will not be robbed, assaulted or even murdered in their beds?"

"No, no, of course I can't, but it's hardly the same, is it?"

"But why not, Roger? Why not? If I take a person who has not got anything and offer him the chance to become a better person, more intelligent, more successful, is that really any different from what happens to almost every human on this planet? Just think how many people risk their lives in jobs every day in order to achieve what I've just said. Roger, we have to do this, don't we?"

He stared straight at me. His eyes seemed somehow bluer, deeper. For a second I was mesmerised. I nodded, then picked up my glass and swallowed the contents in one gulp.

Thoughtfully, I replaced the glass, and, without looking at the Professor, I said, "I can't do anything illegal, you understand that?" I looked at him.

"No, of course not. Nor would I, Roger. Drug companies employ people to test their products; this won't be any different. Those people are aware of the risks. Not only that, but there will be forms – disclaimer forms – which they have to sign. Even hospitals have consent forms."

I agreed with the Professor and said I would look into the legal issues regarding consent forms. We ended our meeting on that note, and I said I would get in touch as soon as I had found anything out.

I spent my free time over the next couple of weeks looking into the use of human guinea pigs for research. I got in touch with the Professor and he asked me to drop into the lab as soon as I could.

The next day found me having a guided tour of the guest suite, which consisted of a bedroom and small bathroom, which had been a couple of storerooms. When I mentioned that he must have been planning this for a while, as the conversion didn't look very new, he explained that he had originally had it converted for his own use, for when he was working late. I noted the windows were fitted with devices to prevent them being opened too far. The Professor showed me the clothes he had obtained, arranged neatly in the whitewood wardrobe.

"No radio or TV," I said.

"No. I want to isolate him from the outside world – no distractions. That's why I've got the clothes. When he gets here I want to try to isolate him from his existing life."

I agreed that the room was fine, and I explained in greater detail than I had on the phone about the forms he would need and I mentioned that it was a more common thing than I previously thought to use humans in research, from simple tasting of new flavours to testing the latest drugs. I told him about one very helpful woman who had told me about a man whose job it was to taste dog and cat food. Apparently, because the pet food was made in a food factory, it had to be fit for human consumption as well. The Professor wasn't convinced, but, as I told him, the woman who told me seemed genuine enough. He took me into his work area and showed me the banks of hard disks and mentioned how many millions of megabytes of storage space he now had, and how much data he had stored away. I tried to give the impression I was interested in all this scientific jargon without sounding too bored.

We went back to the little kitchenette and he made some coffee. He asked how long it would be before I could obtain a body – alive, of course. I explained that I had next week off, so I thought I would give it a try starting on Sunday. I told him I had found a café on the main road outside Tolchester which seemed to be a stopping-off point for tramps and the like journeying north. Both times I had stopped there I had seen a few likely bodies. I think he must have told me 100 times over the next half-hour how anxious he was to get started.

I enquired about Tim, and the Professor assured me that he knew nothing of what we were planning; and he had given Tim three months off so he could visit his parents in Hong Kong. That pleased me as I didn't want the complication of witnesses if things should go wrong. I had started a file on the Professor, and if things went wrong my intention was to pretend I had been helping him in order to obtain evidence.

It was typical: on Sunday, my first day on stake-out at the café, not a single body turned up. Perhaps tramps don't travel on Sundays; perhaps they go to church instead.

Monday started better. I spotted three in the morning. Luckily, I waited before I approached the one I had selected, because all three suddenly got together like long-lost brothers and they left together.

I went into Tolchester and did some shopping and returned to the café late in the afternoon. I had a look round outside – not a soul, so I popped in and had a coffee and cake. I sat there a good hour, but no bodies arrived, so I decided to call it a day and go home after visiting the loo outside.

Having stood and watched my pee fight its way through the mass of fag ends in its bid to reach the sewer, I washed my hands in the heavily stained bowl; but I didn't fancy drying my hands on the grubby-looking towel, so I used my handkerchief. I left the loo and made my way to my car.

I was just about to put the key in the lock when I was startled by a voice from behind me: "Spare the price of a cuppa, Mister."

I turned and looked down. The first thing I noticed, because it was about six inches from my nose, was a grubby hand, palm upwards, covered in places by a ragged mitten.

"Please, Mister." The voice came again, the pleading tone plucking at my heartstrings. Well, that was what it was rehearsed to do.

I looked from the hand at the man's weather-beaten, chubby face, which was contorted into a distressed expression calculated to riddle me with guilt. I took in the hanks of matted hair which erupted from the woollen tea-cosy-type hat on all sides. His brown eyes squinted a message of pain and poverty. His heavy dark-blue overcoat, wrapped over to take up the surplus, was fixed round the middle by what had once been a dress belt. One lapel had been pulled across the chest and secured to the opposite shoulder with a safety pin. His baggy khaki trousers hid whatever (if any) footwear he had on. My nostrils flared as they automatically tested the air, searching for a bad smell which would categorise this person as an outcast – a threat to our false values. His eyes still stared at me. I expected tears to appear at any minute. I watched as the shade of disappointment began to leak into his eyes because he had failed: my hand had not dived towards my pocket in order to rid myself of his presence. I stood firm.

"Look," I said, "I am a writer. I am collecting information for a book I am doing on travellers like yourself. If I buy you a meal in the café," – I pointed with my hand – "could I ask you some questions?"

The outstretched hand was swiftly withdrawn, and the brown eyes were now filled with suspicion and fear. There was now a defiant, guarded look on his face. He took a step back.

"Questions? What sort of questions?" he asked.

"Oh, where have you been? Where are you going? Why do you like the life you lead? – that sort of thing. Nothing to worry about."

"And I get a meal in there free?" He pointed to the café. "No funny business."

"No, no funny business." I held my hands up and half smiled. "I promise."

"What about if I can't answer your questions? What then?"

"Well, you can still have the meal. If you like, you can eat the meal before I ask the questions."

I could see he was mulling it over in his mind. He looked round at the café, then back at me; then I think the hunger pains or the smell from the café, or both, made his mind up, and he agreed.

I led the way, checking he was following into the café. The chap behind the counter showed his displeasure at my new friend. I let him choose what he wanted, then found a table out of the way and we sat down and waited for the food. I asked a few questions. His name was Jack – no, he didn't have a last name; he did once, but he lost it in his travels. I could see he was nervous, looking round all the time. He nearly jumped out of his skin when a voice boomed out that our grub was ready. I went up to the counter to collect the tray.

"Will he need a knife and fork?" the chap asked in a sarcastic tone.

I pretended to take no notice, but made a mental note to come back sometime and introduce myself properly, perhaps check the place over.

I returned to the table and put the plate of steaming sausages, mash and beans in front of Jack – and yes, he did know how to use a knife and fork. I thought he would pounce on the food and devour it like some starving animal, but, although hungry, he ate very slowly, and thoroughly chewed his food – probably a lesson learnt in the past. I waited, watching him; he never looked at me once until he had finished his meal, and he was sipping his mug of tea before I spoke to him again.

He told me he had been on the road as long as he could remember; he didn't remember going to school; as far as he knew he didn't have any family. He started to look agitated when I said that he must have been to school and had a home of some sort, that he must have belonged somewhere to start with, so I changed the subject. I asked him what his future plans were.

"Go here, go there – nothing special" came his answer.

"So it wouldn't matter if you were to stay round here for a while?" I asked.

"Don't know about that. I am only passing through," he said.

"What about if I could offer you a bed and food for a few days?"

"No, no, I can't do any work cos of my back," he whinged.

"No, it wouldn't involve any work; just like now, we would just ask you questions for our research."

He sat there thinking – well, I think that's what he was doing. It was difficult to tell by the expression on his face.

He looked at me. "What about money? Would I get paid?"

I smiled. "Yes, I am sure we can sort something out," I said.

He sat there with that bland expression, probably wondering what else he could ask for.

Before he could say anything, I said, "And we could sort you out with some new clothes – anything like that."

I regretted saying that as soon as I said it because his face changed and he looked at me suspiciously. I realised that it was all right for him to ask for things, but my offering made it look as though I would say anything to get him to do what I wanted; so I sat quietly and waited, wondering if I had blown it.

'Perhaps I should arrest him and take him away in handcuffs,' I thought.

He still sipped his tea. He didn't look directly at me, but I could see he was watching my movements. He was avoiding all eye contact, yet when he had been begging he used his eyes almost as a weapon. So why had he gone all shy now?

My thoughts were interrupted as he put his cup down and, without looking at me, said he would stay just for a couple of days. I tried not to sound too exuberant as I said how pleased I was. I got him another tea and a sticky bun to keep him occupied as I made a call to the Professor. I returned to the table and watched him munching away.

"That's all fixed, Jack. The room is still available."

He didn't seem to take any notice of what I said, but I am sure he was quicker on the uptake than he appeared to be. He had obviously been surviving on his wits for a long time. I thought I would warn the Professor not to be taken in by his appearance. For all I knew he could have been a highly educated man.

He was finally ready to leave, and we made our way towards

my car. I had deliberately parked out of sight of the café so the proprietor wouldn't be able to clock my number plate. I didn't want him reporting what, after all, must have looked a trifle suspicious: a well-dressed man in a new car going off with a tramp.

As we neared the car, Jack suddenly said, "'Old on a mo," and disappeared into the bushes.

I was just about to chase after him when he reappeared clutching a bag – well, more of a blanket tied up with string. I opened up the car and suggested he put his bundle in the boot. I thought that might stop the fleas from getting inside. I don't think he had been in a new car before, and he seemed thrilled by the electric windows. He recoiled when I tried to put the seat belt on him – I think, from his reaction, he thought I was tying him up, so I put mine on first and explained that it was illegal not to wear one.

It didn't take too long to reach the research station. I pipped the horn at the main gates, hoping the Professor had warned the guard. He looked out and I waved. The big gate started to open.

Jack looked amazed. I just hoped he wouldn't notice the high fence around the place.

I drove up to the front of the new building. Good – the Professor was waiting, and thank goodness he wasn't wearing his white coat. I turned the car so Jack would get out facing the Professor, who opened the door and greeted Jack like his long-lost brother. Jack was struggling to undo his belt, so I helped. I looked at his seat as he got out – I was half expecting to see that a flea circus had taken up residence. While the Professor was doing his Dr Livingstone act I retrieved Jack's bundle from the boot. With some effort, due to the weight, I held it at arm's length and passed it to Jack, who held it tight against his stomach as though protecting it from theft. Well, I suppose there could be someone worse off than him who might take a liking to the grubby bundle.

The Professor led Jack inside and I followed. He showed Jack his room. The Professor was behaving completely over the top, even turning the taps on in the bathroom and flushing the loo.

I could see that Jack was getting worried by the Professor's behaviour, so I said, "OK, Jack, we will leave you to settle in. Just make yourself at home. When you are ready, pop down to the kitchen and we can have some tea."

I then grabbed the Professor by the arm and steered him out of the room. I waited until we reached the kitchen before I spoke.

"For goodness' sake, Professor, you're frightening him to death. Just calm down."

"I am sorry, Roger – it's just— Well, I feel so excited. It's like a dream come true."

I popped my head out of the door and looked down the corridor towards Jack's room, expecting to see him making a bolt for it.

Turning back to the Professor, I said, "Well, what do you think of him?"

"He looks all right, Roger. Mind you, a good bath would be an improvement. What's his background?"

"Well, he reckons he has got no family, doesn't remember ever going to school, and has been on the road from the day he was born. I think he must be in his mid-forties. If we could get a surname and date of birth out of him, I could do a check on him."

The Professor looked at me. "He sounds perfect. I wonder if he can read or write."

I shrugged my shoulders. I had never thought to ask – I mean, I automatically assume everybody can read and write (or I did until I moved up here).

We sat talking for a good two hours, then a bleeper went off in the Professor's pocket.

"That's Jack's door," he said.

I quickly put my head out of the door, just in time to see Jack peeping out nervously.

"Hi!" I called. "We are in here." I stood out in the corridor and beckoned him.

He came along looking sheepish. I smiled and ushered him into the kitchen. The Professor was just putting the kettle on, and at least he now tried to behave normally. We got Jack to sit down at the table and joined him. The Professor started his cross-examination. I watched Jack's face, and at any sign of distress or agitation I would butt in and change the subject. At first the Professor looked a bit annoyed at my interruptions, but then he realised what I was up to and followed my example.

The kettle boiled and the Professor made a pot of tea. Just then a phone started to ring in another room somewhere in the building, and the Professor left to answer it.

"What do you think of him?" I asked Jack.

"Blooming well talks a lot, don't he?"

"Yes, I suppose he does, but he is a very nice chap – always helping people, very kind." I piled on the compliments. "He's very pleased you agreed to help us."

"Well, it will be all right for a few days; then I will have to be off," Jack said matter-of-factly.

"Is your room all right?" I asked.

"Suppose so. The bed's no good – too soft. The floor will be better."

The Professor came back. He went to a wall cupboard in the corner and fetched a mug. From a different cupboard he took two cups. I watched him as he poured out the tea. He placed the mug in front of Jack.

"I thought you would prefer a mug, Jack."

He placed a cup in front of me, then brought his own cup and the sugar bowl. He placed the sugar bowl in front of Jack and sat down. "I don't know if you take sugar, Jack. Please help yourself."

We both watched, with some distaste, as he put at least six heaped spoons into his mug and gave it a lazy stir. The Professor and I chatted away, trying to draw Jack into the conversation, but we found it hard work as Jack didn't seem to have much to say – or, indeed, have any opinions about anything. His ignorance – no, it would be nearer the truth to say 'his innocence' – about the world around him was a revelation. After about ten minutes Jack yawned, displaying a mouth full of discoloured teeth.

I said, "You look tired. Do you want to go to bed?"

He seemed to be having trouble keeping his eyes open as he nodded.

I saw him back to his room and returned to the kitchen. The Professor was at the sink, washing the cups.

He turned as I walked in and said, "Is he all right?"

I nodded. "What did you give him?" I asked. He looked at me as if to say, "How did you know?"

"Oh, just a strong sleeping tablet. I must have him relaxed, totally. I'll give him some more sedatives in the morning." I must have looked concerned. "Don't worry, Roger, I know what I am doing. I'll be sleeping in the lab, so I won't be far away."

I looked at my watch. "Well, I might as well go home. I'll come back first thing in the morning." The Professor came to the door with me. We both stopped outside Jack's room and listened. I think we expected to hear him snoring loudly, but it all seemed quiet.

"Do you think he is all right?" I whispered.

The Professor nodded and we carried on. He showed me how to operate the security door, and I left.

I was back early the next morning. I crept quietly past Jack's room – which was a bit silly really because I didn't even know if he was in there or not. I found the Professor in the lab at his desk, which was piled with sheets of paper.

"Have you seen Jack?" I asked.

"I popped in earlier, but he was still sound asleep, so I left him."

We talked generally for a few minutes, then I asked him what he intended to do. He said he wanted to try downloading information into Jack's brain to boost his intelligence and general knowledge.

"Is there a risk that you will damage his brain if you try to put too much data in at once?" I asked.

"No, I don't think so, Roger. I think confusion is more likely than damage."

Just then the bleeper went off in the Professor's pocket.

"Ah, Jack's out and about."

We both hurried from the lab. Jack was standing outside his door, yawning and having a good scratch. We both approached him. He was still wearing the clothes he had been wearing the day before, and he seemed to have slept in them.

"Good morning, Jack. Did you sleep well?" the Professor asked in the kind of voice you might use talking to a three-year-old. "Would you like some breakfast?"

Jack was still looking a mite confused, probably wondering where the hell he was. We led him to the kitchen and sat him down. I sat opposite, smiling at him, trying to reassure him, settle him down. The Professor made himself busy, putting the kettle on, turning the cooker on, putting some bread in the toaster. Jack seemed to be waking up, although it was difficult to tell by his face. The Professor placed a plate in front of Jack – beans on toast. I hoped he liked beans. The Professor had obviously decided he not only liked them but lived on them, judging by the amount he had piled on the plate. Jack seemed to pep up as he looked at the plate in front of him. He was soon tucking in. The Professor brought over the tea and sugar bowl and sat down. He and I chatted between ourselves, trying to draw a response from Jack, but he was too busy eating. I don't think he realised we were there. He did stop eating a couple of times, and looked thoughtful, but then just carried on eating. Finally, when his plate was empty, he pushed it away and sat back in his chair, his mug of tea in his hand.

"Had enough?" the Professor asked.

He nodded. There was no thanks – still, he probably never had much use for manners.

I looked at the Professor, who was watching anxiously as Jack took a sip from his mug. Jack grimaced and leant forward, dumping his mug on the table. The Professor looked horrified.

"Not enough sugar!" wailed Jack, and he proceeded to add another couple of spoonfuls.

The Professor heaved a sigh of relief. I grinned to myself. Jack wouldn't have a clue he was being drugged – the thought would never enter his head. Jack tasted the tea again. Satisfied, he drained the mug in several noisy gulps. We sat in silence, waiting for the drug to take effect. It seemed ages before Jack started to look drowsy. His eyelids started to flutter as he struggled to stay awake. We helped him to his feet and, supporting him between us, we walked him into the lab and settled him on the couch in a semi-reclining position. The Professor asked me to remove his hat. He fetched an instant camera and took several photos of Jack. He placed them on a table to develop, then wheeled a trolley over. He removed the white cover to reveal neat lines of gleaming surgical instruments.

"We have to make an incision for the probe to enter the skull."

The Professor was talking to me as he thought out loud. He asked me stand behind Jack and to hold Jack's head on its side.

"I will make the incision just behind the ear."

He pushed Jack's hair away from the area, and asked me to hold it as I held the head. He then swabbed the area with an antiseptic, then he selected one of the vicious-looking instruments from the tray. I looked away. I could feel the pressure he was using, and had to use quite a lot of effort to keep the head in place.

"That's it," he said as he dropped the instrument back on the trolley. He pointed to the area and said, "See – I've made a tiny hole and fitted a self-sealing membrane."

I looked down. "It's not very big," I commented.

"No, it doesn't have to be. The probe is only slightly bigger than a needle. I've made a small cover, so it will look just like a spot."

"I hope he doesn't decide to squeeze it," I said.

The Professor ignored my remark. "I've numbed the area round the membrane, so he shouldn't feel the need to have a scratch."

"Can I take my hands away now?" I asked.

The mention of the word 'scratch' reminded me that I was probably holding a fleas' nest in my hands. I examined my hands carefully for any signs of creepy-crawlies. The Professor wheeled his trolley away, then came back with another one with a computer on. He switched on and the screen glowed green. He took the top off a clear plastic box and lifted out an object about five inches long. From one end a delicate-looking cable disappeared into the housing at the side of the computer. While I watched he removed a cover from the opposite end to reveal a gold needle, about three inches long. He held it up to show me.

"Is that the probe?" I asked.

"Yes, that's it, Roger. Now can you hold Jack's head again, just as before?"

I pulled the hair out of the way, and clamped the head as tightly as I could. The Professor dipped the probe in a jar of colourless liquid. I watched as he bent over Jack, the light fixed to his forehead highlighting the area of the incision. When I saw he was just about to push the probe in, I looked away. My fingers trembled, and I felt the cold sweat in my armpits.

"Won't he feel any pain?" I asked.

"No, not at all. The brain is completely insensitive to pain. In fact, in the past I've put the probe into a chimp's brain when he has been awake."

"Really?" I said.

"Right, it's in place now, so try and keep his head as still as possible."

I looked down. All that was visible was a small black box with the wire coming out. The Professor pulled a chair over and started to tap away at the keyboard. He then sat back and put his hands behind his head.

"The program is running all right. It will take about ten minutes."

"What does the program actually do?" I asked.

"Well, it establishes Jack's brain pattern. I need to know the pattern before I can put any data in. During the time I was working with chimps I realised that something was blocking what I was trying to put in. I found in the end that the brain was running a sort of defensive shield, blocking any data entering other than what came through the normal channels. Anyway, I found the source of the blockage and discovered a way to get round it. In fact, I can now add my own shield to prevent anyone else adding data. I don't know if the human brain has a similar defensive shield, but Jack's brain pattern should tell me if there is likely to be a problem downloading."

The Professor turned back to his computer and started tapping the keys again. My hands were getting tired. I relaxed my grip, one hand at a time and flexed my fingers. I looked down at Jack. I could see from his chest moving that he was still breathing. What would I do if he stopped – certainly not mouth-to-mouth.

My thoughts were interrupted: "That's finished now," said the Professor as he pushed the trolley away and stood up.

He leant over Jack and slowly pulled the probe out. I watched fascinated. I expected a jet of brain matter to spurt out of the hole – but there was nothing. The Professor carefully cleaned the probe in the clear liquid and replaced the cover before putting the probe back in its box. He then picked up something I couldn't see with a pair of tweezers and leant over Jack again.

"There! What do you think?"

I leant down and looked.

"Bloody marvellous!" I said, looking at him with a smile on my face. "As you said, it looks just like a spot. Can I let go now?"

"Yes," the Professor replied.

I gently turned the head upright, and with a sigh stood back.

"What now?" I asked.

"We just wait until he starts to wake up; then we can put him back in his own room."

I walked over to where the Professor was tapping away at the keyboard.

"I'll be glad when this antiquated thing has been replaced," he mumbled.

I stood and watched for a few minutes. I was starting to feel like a spare part. I scratched behind my ear, just to check there were no spots. Something was bugging me. I looked over at Jack. I walked over and looked down at him. He was still breathing. I leant over and looked closely at his face.

"You know, Professor, I noticed when I was holding his head that, although he has a mop of hair on his head and he doesn't shave, there's no stubble." I gently ran my fingers over his chin as I spoke.

I looked over to the Professor and realised I had been talking to myself; he was totally absorbed in what he was doing. I looked down at the rest of Jack's body, noticing the gentle rhythm of his chest as it rose and fell. I thought for a moment, then I carefully pulled up the baggy multicoloured jumper, undid the buttons on the check shirt and pulled it open. I stared for a moment, then I turned to the Professor.

"You'd better come and see this."

Something in the tone of my voice stopped him working and he looked up at me. He got up and came over and looked down at Jack.

"Good God!" he exclaimed. "How on earth? It's a woman!"

"Yes, you are right there," I said as I looked yet again at the pair of lovely firm round breasts as they rose and fell.

A feeling of guilt suddenly flooded over me and I leant down and did the shirt up and pulled the jumper down. I expected Jack to suddenly wake up and scream rape. We both backed away to the other side of the room.

"What should we do now?" I whispered.

We both stood staring over at the figure lying on the couch.

He at last broke the silence: "Nothing."

I looked at him enquiringly.

"Nothing?" I repeated.

"Yes," he said. "We just carry on. It doesn't matter, male or female. In some ways it couldn't be better."

"How do you make that out?" I asked.

"Well, all the data I have is more suitable for a man, but that's no problem. Roger, we wanted an opposite, but it never occurred to me to have the opposite sex. Just think: a women who thinks and behaves like a man! It's an exciting challenge. Just think: we could take data from Jack's brain and give it to a man."

I could see from the sparkle in the Professor's eyes that it would be a waste of time my arguing. Mind you, what would I argue about? As the Professor said, what difference did it make? I sat on the table and watched Jack, while the Professor messed about with his computer.

Fifteen minutes went by and I noticed Jack was beginning to stir. I called the Professor and we walked him (or should I say 'her'?) back to the kitchen and sat her down. I stood by her side, supporting her, while the Professor put the kettle on. She finally opened her eyes and the Professor started talking to me just as he had been when we first took her out. She looked around, a little puzzled.

"Another cup of tea, Jack?" the Professor said, putting the mug down in front of her.

She lifted her hand up to her head. "I feel a bit dizzy," she said.

"Probably all that food," I joked. "Tell you what: drink your tea and I will take you out for a walk. Perhaps you've been stuck indoors too long."

That seemed to perk her up a bit. I looked at the Professor, who gave a little nod of approval.

The tea finished, I took her out into the grounds. She took a few deep breaths.

"Feeling better now?" I asked.

She nodded.

"I can tell you don't like being cooped up, but, don't worry – it's not for long, then you can be on your way."

We walked along in silence.

I suddenly thought, 'What happens when the Professor has finished? What will happen to her then? I hadn't given that a thought before. I made a mental note to ask him.

"Jack, have you ever been married?" I asked.

"No – got no time for that sort of thing," she replied. "Of course, some of the people on the road do get married sometimes, and I've watched them posh dos they have in churches – good pickings they are."

"How do you mean?" I asked.

"Well, you hang about at the back of the church hall and there's always tons of food being chucked out."

"Yes, I suppose there is. Tell me, Jack: do you ever think about settling down? I mean, one day you will be too old to wander about. What will you do then?"

She didn't answer.

I thought to myself, 'I wonder where tramps go when they are too old.'

We made our way back inside the building. My stomach was informing me that we had missed lunch, so I was pleased that in our absence the Professor had made some sandwiches. We all sat round the table like a little family. The Professor gave Jack a special mug and we soon had her tucked up in bed.

We went back into the lab. The Professor said that, if he worked all evening, he should have the data ready in the morning.

"Tell me," I said: "what sort of things are you going to input?" I don't know why, but it seemed important for me to know.

"Well, Roger, I've given that a lot of thought while you were out walking. I think, apart from making her more intelligent and improving her general knowledge, I want to try to change her values. Basically, I'm going to try to make her the direct opposite of what she is now."

"But, Professor, won't she notice such radical change?"

"No, I don't think so. My expectation is that everything will seem normal and natural to her."

"Another thing, Professor: when your new data contradicts existing data, which will be the data she acts on? I mean, you as good as said that's what could have happened with Susan."

"Yes, I agree, but with Susan we only took data out. In Jack's case, I intend not only to erase existing data and add new data, but I shall give the brain information to substantiate the new data."

"OK, Professor, you say you will erase the existing data, but what about the basic data – you know, the data that tells the brain to move a leg or arm, go to the loo – that sort of thing? How can you be sure you won't erase that as well?"

"A good point, Roger. There is a small chance of losing data of that kind, but I am confident that the brain will quickly relearn those things if it needs to."

We talked on for a while, and I realised I was starting to get silly, trying to catch the Professor out. I couldn't think why I was behaving like that, so I made an excuse and left for home.

The next morning was a repeat of the previous morning. Jack was drugged and we connected her up, and downloaded, as the Professor called it. I watched with apprehension as I held her head. I could swear her head was swelling up as the data was transferred.

'My God,' I thought, 'what if her brain explodes!'

I realised I had not checked that the Professor had got Jack to sign disclaimers. It seemed like a lifetime before the Professor was satisfied and began the disconnecting procedure. I heaved a sigh of relief as I let go of her head. Now we would have to wait. I saw the Professor preparing a syringe.

"What's that?" I asked.

"I want her to stay under for a while – keep her relaxed so that her brain can devote all its time to absorbing and sorting the new data."

The Professor produced a stretcher and we took Jack back to her room and put her to bed.

"How long will she be out?" I asked.

"Some hours yet. Could you make us some lunch? I want to do some more work," said the Professor.

I was grateful to have something to do. While I was preparing the lunch I kept popping in to see how Jack was. She seemed to be sleeping peacefully, showing no signs of the turmoil which might have been raging in her head.

The Professor and I ate our lunch in silence. Perhaps he was more worried than he showed.

After lunch he went back to his work. I found a paperback and went and sat in Jack's room.

It was about four in the afternoon when she started to stir. I wasn't sure whether to go and fetch the Professor, or stay. I thought she might fall out of bed or something, so I decided to stay. I watched as she moved in the bed. What if she woke up mad, and started leaping round the room, screaming? The memory of when I was a green young copper trying to deal with a man having an epileptic fit, and the mess I made of that, suddenly entered my mind. Perhaps I should have had a tranquilliser gun. Jack's movements were becoming more and more frequent.

Suddenly she sat up, rubbing her eyes. She spotted me.

"What are you doing here?" she asked.

"We were worried about you, so I was just making sure you were all right. How are you feeling?"

She stuck her tongue out. "Yuck! My mouth feels drier than a duck in an oven."

"Would you like a cup of tea?" I asked.

"God, yes," she replied.

"I'll go and make you one in the kitchen. Come along when you are ready."

I left the room and paused in the corridor to take a deep breath. Well, she looked all right.

I had just put the kettle on when the Professor came in.

"Oh, I thought Jack was up – the bleeper." He tapped his pocket.

"Oh," I said. "No, that was me."

The bleeper only worked when someone left the room, so he didn't know I had gone in there.

"I've been sitting with her, but now she has woken up. I am making her a cuppa. She will be along soon."

"How did she seem?" the Professor asked.

"Well, OK. That is as far as I could tell, but she was still in bed when I left her, so . . ." I shrugged my shoulders.

The Professor said he would come back when he heard the bleeper again as he was just in the middle of something tricky.

I had made the tea and poured it out, but there was still no sign of Jack. I was getting a bit worried and was out in the corridor on my way back to her room when she appeared.

"I was just coming to tell you your tea was ready."

We went back to the kitchen together.

I pointed to her mug. "I haven't put any sugar in," I said.

She sat down, then the Professor came in.

"Are you all right, Jack?" he asked.

"Yes, fine. Well, I feel a bit woozy. I've probably being inside too much."

The Professor and I drank our tea and watched Jack's every move, but she seemed the same to me. Perhaps the transfer had gone wrong or something.

Jack finished her tea and got up and put the empty cup in the sink and said, "I think I will have a bath; I feel a bit grubby."

"OK, see you later for tea," I said.

We stood in silence until we heard her door close; then the Professor turned to me, eyes sparkling.

"Well, what do you think?" he asked.

"It hasn't worked," I said. "She is still the same."

"What about wanting a bath?" the Professor asked.

"Well, perhaps she has a bath once a year and today's the day," I answered.

The Professor walked over to the sink and picked up Jack's mug.

"Did you put any sugar in?"

"No, I left it for her to do," I replied.

"Look." He showed me the empty mug. "No trace of sugar, and she didn't wash the mug out."

"So?" I said.

"Jack always has at least six spoons of sugar, and there is always quite a bit left in the mug. Part of the new data included instructions not to use sugar in her tea!"

Feeling embarrassed that I hadn't noticed these changes, especially as I would have normally, I tried to bluster. "Perhaps she's just tired or confused. Two small changes, if that's what they are, don't mean she's a new woman," I argued.

The Professor looked disappointed by my doubts. "All right, Roger, we will just have to watch her and note any changes, no matter how small, then I can compare them with my program."

I nodded. I told him I would prepare some sandwiches for tea, and he went back to the lab.

He came back about forty-five minutes later.

"No sign yet?" he said.

"No – I suppose she is all right. Do you think I should check?"

"No," said the Professor. "Let's give her a bit longer. Perhaps she is enjoying a long soak."

About ten minutes later the bleeper went off in the Professor's pocket, and a few minutes later Jack appeared at the kitchen door. Well, at first glance she looked the same, but then I realised that was only the clothes. She had washed her hair, and she had even combed it, and it looked nice. Her face looked softer – definitely cleaner. I think her eyes looked brighter, but I was looking for changes now, almost willing her to be different, probably noticing things that I hadn't bothered with before.

"Feeling better now?" asked the Professor.

"Yes, thanks. I'm starving hungry, though," she replied.

"Come and sit down. I've done some sandwiches," I said.

She joined us at the table, and we attacked the food. We talked as we ate, and Jack joined in the conversation – something she had never done before. In fact, we had quite an enjoyable meal. After we had washed up I asked Jack if she would like to go for a walk.

"Yes," she replied with a smile – which was another first.

CHAPTER 10

Out in the grounds we walked in silence for a while. I waited for her to speak. She suddenly stopped and crossed her arms and said, "This world's such a beautiful place, don't you think?"

"Yes, I suppose it is," I replied.

I studied her face as she looked into the distance. It was certainly softer, as if she had washed away the years of hardness she had acquired on the road. She didn't have a pretty face, but her skin was good and her teeth were looking whiter, so she was obviously cleaning them. I wondered if she had ever been to a dentist, and that made me wonder about doctors: where do tramps go when they are ill? I mean, I've never seen tramps in a doctor's surgery.

My thoughts were halted by Jack: "Have you travelled to many places in the world?" she asked.

"Oh, only the usual package holidays: Spain, Italy, France," I replied.

"I would like to see those countries one day," she said with a faraway look in her eyes.

I asked her if she could remember anything about her past. She looked puzzled by that question, so I quickly changed the subject. Later, as we returned to the building, she suddenly said she could remember that she had a happy childhood until her parents had been killed in a car crash, and she had been left on her own.

Back in the kitchen the Professor made us some drinks, and soon afterwards Jack said she was tired and went to bed.

We went through to the lab, and the Professor asked how our walk went. I told him she was certainly more chatty; she seemed brighter, more alive, and asked a lot of questions. I told him what she had said about her parents. He beamed at that, and got quite excited as he told me that was a clear indication his program was working, as he had programmed exactly that fact. I felt like telling him that it was also possible that was what did happen to her parents, but I kept quiet. The Professor told me he had found a case of women's clothes and a make-up case in his storeroom. He explained that they had been left behind by one of his visitors a while ago. He said she had left in rather a hurry, but he didn't explain why, and I didn't ask. He said he had put the clothes in Jack's room.

"Professor, there's something I have been wondering about: if you change a person's mind, will that change his physical characteristics as well? I mean, say you give a clumsy person the mind of an expert painter, will he become an expert, or will he become confused because in his mind he can do it, but physically he can't?"

The Professor thought for a while. "Well, Roger, I honestly don't know. I don't know if a clumsy person is clumsy because of a faulty brain or if a person's physical limitations are a separate issue, but I think we should look into it. It might open up a lot of new possibilities."

I thought afterwards I should have kept quiet, as I could just see him giving me a shopping list for specific bodies.

The next morning I was there at the usual time. I glanced at the door to Jack's room on the way past. I found the Professor in the kitchen.

"She's not up yet?" I asked.

"No, not yet," he replied.

We had a cup of tea and sat there talking. The time was dragging on, and I asked if he had the bleeper switched on. He checked his pocket.

"Damn!" he said. "It's in my other coat in the lab. I had better fetch it."

"Morning." A voice spoke behind us, making us both jump.

We turned towards the door. Jack was standing in the doorway, although her resemblance to the Jack we first knew was, to say the least, minimal. This Jack was a woman, five foot five inches tall, of medium build, with short, dark hair and brown eyes. My police-trained mind automatically noted her description. She was wearing a peach-coloured dress. The pale-orange lipstick was a little overdone, but she looked twenty years younger, and, although you wouldn't call her beautiful, she was certainly attractive in a very desirable way.

"What are you two gawping at?" she asked as she swept into the room. Neither of us spoke; we were too busy closing our mouths, which had been hanging open. She started looking through the cupboards. I would have asked her what she was looking for if I had been able to tear my gaze from her curvy bottom, which wiggled as she reached up to open the doors. The dress was a little bit tight, and it rode up her hips, displaying the backs of her thighs. I glanced at the Professor, who was, judging by the way his eyes were leaping from their sockets, not thinking of scientific facts just at that moment.

"Ah, coffee! I fancy a change this morning," Jack said as she turned from the cupboard, proudly displaying the jar in her hand.

The Professor and I were completely stuck for what to say. Before, although we knew she was a woman, we coped because we still treated her like a man; but now it was as if she was making a statement that she was a woman. So what should I say? Should I ignore how she looked and carry on talking to her as I did before? Should we discuss the change or act like nothing had happened? I decided just to carry on as before and not mention it unless Jack brought it up. Perhaps the Professor was right and she didn't remember what she was like before. Perhaps she believed she had always been like this.

She made her coffee and joined us at the table. We both smiled at her. The Professor asked how she was, and talked about the weather. For the first time I noticed her hands – mainly because of the splash of colour of the nail varnish she was wearing. She must have scrubbed her hands. Gone were the thin lines of grime around her nails and in the skin creases. She had short, stubby fingers, and I thought she needed a few rings in order to make it clear that they were a woman's fingers. She finished her coffee.

"What have you got planned for today?" she asked. Before we could answer, she carried on: "I would like to do some shopping. There are some things I need."

I looked at the Professor. I could see the alarm in his eyes.

"Well, if you make a list, I can get them for you," I said.

"I would rather go myself, please." I could see that the Professor hadn't erased her talent for begging. Before I had a chance to think, I was agreeing to take her into Tolchester.

"Oh, thanks, Roger. I'll go and get ready."

The Professor waited until he heard Jack's door close; then: "That was a bit silly, Roger." The anger rattled his voice.

"I had to say something. She was getting upset. She might have wanted to leave." I was almost pleading, which made me angry.

"All right, but you must watch her all the time. Never let her out of your sight for a second," he said. "Oh, you can be sure of that," I said with a smirk on my face.

The Professor gave me a hard look. "While you are gone I'll get the next set of data ready and we can download in the morning."

I looked at him sharply. "So soon? Shouldn't we wait a bit longer?" I asked.

"No, I don't see why. She seems to be coping, wouldn't you say?"

"Yes, it's remarkable. It's just— Well, OK."

I wanted to say she was fine as she was, but I didn't want to get into an argument. I felt worried, protective. What if we overdid it? What if something went wrong? This was all going through my mind, but my concerns were all soon forgotten as Jack came back, wearing a biscuit-coloured topcoat and carrying a black handbag. The coat fitted better than the dress had, and she looked quite smart. She stood in the doorway.

"I was wondering about money. You said you would pay me for helping you."

"Yes, of course," the Professor said as he got his wallet out.

He handed her four tens, which she folded and put away in her bag. I would have expected the old Jack to look in amazement at what to her would have been a fortune.

I walked Jack to my car and I noticed that she tackled the seat belt just as if she had been doing it all her life. We drove away from the lab. I was tempted just to drive away and not come back. I could expose the Professor's work and save Jack from any further treatment. I was sure the Professor was worried that I might do just that, judging by the way he looked at me as we left.

We spent a pleasant few hours round the shops. Jack seemed so happy, and I really enjoyed being with her. We even had lunch in a burger bar, which, believe it or not, was my first time ever, and I enjoyed it. Jack spent the Professor's money and the same amount of mine. I tried to keep a note of what she bought, but I gave up after a while. The pile of parcels and bags I was carrying just seemed to keep growing. I did note that she didn't buy a new woolly hat or knapsack, which would have led me to suspect that she was getting ready to leave us.

She was starting to look tired, so I suggested we go back. The drive back took a lot of effort on my part, but my professional training finally won and it wasn't too long before I was pulling up outside the lab. The Professor was waiting outside the door and greeted us like long-lost friends – a reminder of when I first brought Jack there. He helped me to carry Jack's purchases to her room and we left her to sort them out.

Back in the kitchen, he showed me the bleeper, so that I knew that Jack couldn't surprise us again.

"Well, how did it go?" he asked. "You were gone a very long time," the Professor said.

"Well, you know what women are like when they are shopping – no sense of time. Anyway, it went fine. I kept an eye on what she bought – no wire-cutters or tunnelling equipment." I tried to sound as sarcastic as possible.

The Professor took no notice.

"Come into the lab a minute," he said.

I followed him. From behind his desk he fetched a black dustbin liner, which he held up with a great grin on his face.

"Look," he said as he placed it on the floor in front of me and opened it.

I leant forward to see the contents, and the stale smell soared up and hit my nose, making me snap my head back. I looked enquiringly at the Professor, who seemed not to notice the smell.

"Her old clothes," he said excitedly. "She's thrown them away – her link with the past."

"Oh, I see," I replied. I obviously didn't share his enthusiasm.

"I found the bag in her room, while you were out."

I frowned at him. "Have you been poking about in her room?" My angry response took him by surprise, and he looked frightened for a second. He then recovered his composure and gave me a hard look. I looked away. I felt angry. The thought of him looking through her things churned my stomach. I had also lost my self-control and betrayed my personal feelings. Despite all my years of training, I had let this rut of a man get through my defences. I tried to cover up by asking questions about what he had been doing while we were away, but the atmosphere was now tense between us. It was a relief when the bleeper went off in his pocket, acting as a signal for us to make our way back to the kitchen.

Jack was already there, busy looking through the cupboards. She turned at our entry and smiled – at me first; I was sure of that. We all pitched in and made a meal.

We sat and talked as we ate. I was aware that the Professor was watching Jack and me whenever we were talking to each other, but I was determined not to let him intimidate me. After all, I was only making sure Jack was happy and relaxed.

After we had cleared away, Jack said she was tired and went to bed. I made my excuses and left.

I had a very fretful night's sleep, and I seemed to have been asleep for only a few minutes before I woke. It took me a while to work out who I was and where I was, then to realise I had not set (or had missed) the alarm. It was an hour later than my normal time for rising. I cursed and had a quick shower and shave.

My mouth felt dry and sore as I drove to the lab. I rubbed my chin; the stubble I had missed while shaving itched a bit. My eyes felt tender.

"Damn! Damn!" I thumped the steering wheel in anger. I wanted to look and feel my best.

Then I couldn't open the security door, and had to ring the bell. At last the door was opened by the Professor.

"I didn't think you were coming," he said.

"I'm here now," I snapped back.

'Nothing like getting off to a good start,' I thought.

He explained that Jack had woken up early, so he had put her in the lab already. As I entered the room I noticed Jack, in her usual sitting position on the couch. I walked over to her. Two wide straps encased her body. I looked at her looking so peaceful, her chest moving gently. I leant down and picked up the loose end of one of the straps and rubbed it through my fingers. The Professor came over.

"I had to put the straps on to stop her falling off."

I nodded.

I wondered what else he had been doing – probably had his hand up her skirt.

"Are you ready, Roger?" he asked.

I nodded and moved to my usual position behind her head.

I looked down at her. With a sigh I gently turned her head, then drew the palm of my hand slowly across her cheek and brushed her hair out of the way. I looked away, gritting my teeth, as the Professor inserted the probe. I watched him as he worked the keyboard.

'It's funny how you can suddenly take a dislike to someone,' I thought; 'but then, our relationship has always been more professional than friendly.'

I found that subconsciously, as I stood there, I had been caressing Jack's head with my fingers, probably trying to reassure her, to let her know I was there. What would she think if she knew what we were doing to her, and, in fact, had already done to her?

"Oh, by the way, Professor, I will have to go as soon as we have put her back in her room. I've got to be in court and I expect it will go on all afternoon."

"Hmm, that should be all right, but can you leave a number in case I need to get in touch?"

I nodded.

It was a good thirty minutes before he disconnected the equipment. We didn't speak during that time. While he was packing away, I walked round and faced Jack. What the hell were we doing, violating her brain? What turmoil had we just unleashed into that innocence? I realised I had not got to know the old Jack, and I wondered whether I would have liked her as much as I did the new one. That question, I knew, would never be answered.

I turned to the Professor: "Her childhood – will she remember it?" I asked.

"Oh, yes, but not the one she actually experienced. I've given her a completely new one."

"But why? Why did you have do that?" I asked with a disgusted look on my face.

"Roger, you must understand, you just can't add a new middle or later life; it has to be linked with an earlier life. There has to be continuity. Look at it this way: if we gave her a new identity for only the last twenty years, all her earlier memories would seem disconnected; so she would become bewildered and frightened. Her memories would be thrown into confusion. It would be like recording over a song on a tape without erasing the previous one – you would end up with a distortion of both recordings." What he said made sense.

"But you have still got the data relating to her first life, haven't you?" I asked him.

"Yes, it's stored away," he replied.

"Well, couldn't that data be turned into pictures?" I asked.

"Yes, it could, but it would take years, and what would be the point? She wouldn't remember any of it, so it would be meaningless to her," he replied; then he went back to his toys.

I bit my lip. What if she did remember, or want to remember? What if trying to remember was like looking into a black hole, a void? Wouldn't that be just as frightening?

My deep thoughts were interrupted by a hushed moan from Jack. The Professor came over and we undid the straps. Then, supporting her between us, we took her back to her room. We laid her on the bed, and the Professor took a syringe from the dressing table and injected a colourless liquid into her slender arm. I covered her with a blanket, tucking it under her chin. I gently stroked her cheek with my fingers, and tried to wipe away a small, dark smudge of eye make-up that was staining the side of her nose. I looked guiltily at the Professor, but he hadn't noticed. He was too busy packing his instruments up.

We left the room together. I checked my watch.

"I had better be going," I said as I took a card from my pocket and scribbled a number on the back. "That's where I'll be; I should be home by six, though." I passed him the card.

He went with me to the door. Things were definitely frosty between us, and I took a deep breath when I got outside. I made my way to the court, stopping only to buy a sandwich for my lunch.

While I waited for my case to come up, I sat there thinking. I made up my mind to get Jack away from the lab as soon as I could. She could stay with me – she would have her own room. I could look after her – take her on holiday wherever she wanted to go. I smiled as I thought of her on a plane, probably for the first time. Then I frowned. Perhaps in her new identity she was used to flying. I suddenly realised how little I actually knew about her. I decided to ask the Professor to give me a list of what she now knew.

The court case was a waste of my entire afternoon as the defendant changed his plea to guilty, but I had an enjoyable evening, mainly spent planning for Jack's arrival. I went to bed feeling happy and pleased.

I was still feeling happy when I arrived at the lab the next morning. I even managed the security door. I could hear the sound of voices and laughter coming from the kitchen, and I quickened my pace.

I entered the room and said good morning with a smile on my face. My eyes focused on Jack, who was standing by the sink. The smile drained from my face and was replaced by a cold, sinking feeling when I noticed the dark, unfriendly look she gave me before she looked away. I looked at the Professor.

"Morning, Roger," he greeted me.

I deliberately looked at Jack, who was staring at the floor, then back at the Professor, my look demanding an explanation. The silence was heavy and awkward. I didn't know what to say. Something had gone wrong with the programming. I felt the anger welling up inside me.

'We should have stopped,' I thought.

Jack suddenly spoke. Looking at the Professor, she said, "I think I will go to my room. I feel tired"

The Professor nodded.

I watched her face as she left. She didn't look at me once, but just stared at the floor. I stood rooted to the spot, my fists clenched with the tension I was feeling. The Professor cleared the table and started to wash up.

As soon as I heard Jack's door close, I walked over to him.

"Well?"

He looked at me.

"What's gone wrong?" I demanded.

"I am not sure, Roger. She seemed all right until you came in; then her mood changed. I am sure it's only temporary – probably a reaction to the data. Perhaps we overdid it." He shrugged his shoulders. "Don't worry – it will sort itself out. Just give it time."

The Professor's reassurances didn't make me feel any better. I could feel something was wrong.

I stayed for lunch, but Jack's attitude towards me seemed to get worse. She ignored everything I said, even when I spoke about the shopping trip. I thought, if anything could, that would spark some interest from her, some comment – but there was nothing. As far as she was concerned, the Professor was the only other person there. And he didn't help. He could have made an effort to include me in the conversation.

After lunch, when I decided to go home, I tackled him about it as he saw me to the door. He said I was seeing things that weren't there, and he told me not to worry so much; things would look different in the morning.

I drove home in exactly the opposite mood to the one I had arrived in. At home I took a bottle and sat brooding in the room I had selected for Jack. I just couldn't understand it. It had to be the last lot of sodding data. There must have been a confliction with the previous lot – but why me? Why not the Professor? Why not both of us? Could it be that I reminded her of someone from her past – someone who had harmed her?

I decided I would get the Professor to program her to like me – to love me. That would be the answer.

Somehow I must have got into bed, because the next thing I was waking up with a thumping headache and a mouth that felt as though it was full of sawdust.

It was nearly ten thirty before I felt safe to venture out and drive to the lab. I was feeling reasonably cheerful. My late arrival would give Jack more time, I thought. After all, women were usually at their worst first thing in the morning.

I parked the car and was just about to enter the lab when I heard the sound of voices coming from round the side of the building; so I made my way round the corner. I spotted Jack and the Professor walking away from me. Jack looked happy, judging by the way she was swinging along. The sound of her laughter floated through the still air like a transparent cloud to be sucked into my waiting ears. My hopes rose as I walked after them. As I got closer, my happy thoughts turned to anger. They were behaving like a happy couple out for a stroll. A feeling of jealousy cut clean through my self-control. They were so engrossed with each other that I was just a few feet away before they turned as one to face the intruder. I tried to smile at Jack, but just grimaced. Jack's face showed her fear of me, and she instinctively moved behind the Professor for protection.

The Professor greeted me and I stopped directly in front of him and confronted him with my anger and aggression. We stood facing each other like gladiators waiting to do battle. Neither of us spoke for what seemed an eternity, then the Professor turned to Jack and asked her to pop back inside as he wanted to talk to me. She hurried away without a glance at me. I saw the fear in her face as she went past.

I spoke first: "What's going on, Professor? Don't tell me nothing, because I'm not blind or stupid." I stabbed his chest with my finger as I spoke, just to make sure he knew I meant business.

He put his hand up and rubbed the place I had poked him.

"Steady on, Roger. Calm down. I can assure you there is nothing going on. I'm trying to sort it out right now. That's why I was talking to Jack when you arrived. I've been up most of the night checking the data, and I think I may have the answer. Look – let's go into the lab and discuss it."

We walked back in silence. I felt guilty for the way I had behaved. I could hardly blame Jack for being frightened of me if I behaved like a madman. I followed the Professor. I glanced into the kitchen as we passed, but Jack must have been in her room.

In the lab the Professor sat behind his desk and I sat in front.

"Look, Professor – I've got a gut feeling about this. She was getting on well with me right up till you put the last lot of data in, so what exactly did that data consist of?" I asked accusingly.

"Well . . ." He fumbled for words.

"Well?" I asked again.

"Just a few loose ends – improvements." He looked uncomfortable as he spoke.

"Are you sure you didn't instruct her to hate me for some reason? It has occurred to me that you might have done that to prove a point."

"No, of course not!" he retorted, his face reddened with anger at my accusation.

I was feeling better now that he had lost his composure.

"Let me warn you, Professor, if I find out you have deliberately turned her against me, I'll expose your whole operation. I've got it all written down: dates, times – everything."

He looked frightened. He stood up and leant forward across his desk. His eyes were blazing with indignation. He went to say something, then changed his mind. He sat down and his expression changed – softened.

"Roger, don't be a fool. You can't destroy my work, not on a silly whim. Be sensible. I've told you before that there are areas I don't yet fully understand. It's possible that you remind her of someone in her past – someone who has harmed her." The Professor was regaining his composure; his voice was steady again.

"I've already thought of that," I snapped; "but you said you had

120

removed her past, so how could that happen?"

"It's possible I missed something. Roger, surely you can see the possibility!" He was almost pleading.

I got up.

"I don't know, Professor. I am not sure – not convinced by a long way. I need to think about it."

"Where are you going?" he asked, looking concerned.

"To the loo."

I left the room and locked myself in the loo. I stared into the mirror; a stranger glared back. I took several deep breaths and tried to control myself. The past thirty minutes had really shaken me to the core. Never before had I felt so wild inside, so primitive. I could easily have smashed the place up. I held my hands up in front of my face; they were trembling. I leant against the wall and squeezed my eyes closed, so all I could see was the blackness, and slowly the anger began to diminish. I opened my eyes and blinked to clear the mist.

'Think!' I told myself. 'Think! The Professor can put it right – you know he can. I have to butter him up, apologise, crawl. That is it – problem solved!'

I realised I was sweating as I felt a cold tickle run down my side. Opening my shirt, I dried my armpits with some loo paper; then I held my hands under the cold tap and absorbed the refreshing feeling as the temperature in my hands dropped. I returned to the lab a different man.

The Professor was sitting at his desk, drinking from a cup. He smiled as I entered.

"Look, Roger – I am sorry about this misunderstanding. I am sure I can put things right. Just be patient."

"Yes, I am sorry too," I replied as I sat down.

"Help yourself to a cup of tea. I've only just made it." He gestured towards the tray on his desk.

Grateful for something to do, I poured a cup and helped myself to a couple of biscuits. I sat back in my chair and dunked my biscuits and sipped my tea. I listened as the Professor outlined the next part of his program. As I sat there I found his voice becoming a drone – a distant drone.

I heard him say, "Does that sound all right, Roger?"

I felt like I was floating. Did I answer? I listened carefully, head on one side, trying to pick up the words, but they wouldn't register; they wouldn't join together; they wouldn't make a sentence. I looked at the Professor, but he wouldn't stay still. He kept moving from side to side. I could feel a pressure on the sides of my head, like when your eyes are straining. I tried to get up, but nothing was working. It all felt like a dream. I could see Jack's smiling face and I smiled back.

"Come on, Roger – come and have a lie-down." I could hear the voice, but I couldn't see where it was coming from.

My eyes were closed. They were so heavy. I couldn't feel anything. My legs, my arms – where were they? Why weren't they there? I couldn't understand.

"There you are. Lie on the couch. You will soon feel better."

Where was I? The lab, the couch – what was happening? My God, he's going to program me! I tried to scream, but the silence echoed back at me. I couldn't move. I was a mind in a carcass.

The voice came at me again: "Now, don't worry, Roger, all your worries will soon be gone. You know, that was a very silly thing to do, to threaten me like that. You were quite right, though: I did program Jack to hate you. It worked very well, don't you think? You gave me no choice. I could see you were falling in love with her. Next you would have been wanting to take her away from me. No, I couldn't allow that. No, Roger, she's mine. She'll do anything I ask." The voice rambled on through the mist. "Just think, Roger: we can have children – virgin minds! I can work on them as soon as they are born. My very own supply of research material! Now I am going to give you a shot under your arm so they won't spot the mark – you won't feel anything – then I am afraid it's goodbye, Roger. There, that didn't hurt, did it? Such a waste! Still, I don't really need you now."

* * * * *

I sat on my desk as I looked over at Roger. 'Five minutes should be enough,' I thought as I looked at my watch.

I put the cups back on the tray and went through to the kitchen, and I washed the cups and teapot out with boiling water. I grinned to myself. I bet he never thought for one minute he was pouring out his own death warrant. I suppose you could almost call it suicide – administered by his own hand, milord. I chuckled. Of course I could have programmed him, but that would have been awkward, what with his job. My research still had a long way to go, so I decided not to take the risk. I checked my watch and returned to the lab. I checked Roger's pulse and listened to his chest. Satisfied he was dead, I folded the plastic sheet I had put on the couch over him and, using the dreaded brown plastic parcel tape, I taped my parcel up. Finished, I stood back and admired my handiwork. He looked quite good, like a mummy, only this one wouldn't be coming back to life. I left the lab and went to Jack's room, knocking before I entered.

"Ah, there you are, my dear. Are you all right?"

"Yes, Edward. Has that nasty man gone yet?"

"Now, don't worry about him. He can't hurt you ever again, but I need your help to take him away. Now, don't worry – he can't hurt you now. Wait here and I'll be back in a minute."

I left her and went and found Roger's car. Using the keys I had taken from his pocket, I drove it on the grass round to the back of the lab and parked it as close to the fire door as I could. I then had a look in the boot and the glovebox and under the seat – nothing interesting. I then went back in through the front door and collected Jack. We went through to the lab. Seeing the bundle on the couch, Jack cowered against me.

"Don't worry, my love – he can't hurt you. I promise."

I went over to the fire door and pushed it open. I had a look round outside. Satisfied, I returned to the couch and pulled it across the floor until it was as near the fire door as possible. I went over to Jack, who was standing next to my desk.

"Come on, my dear – I want you to hold the bottom and help me get him in the car; then we can take him away."

I led her over to the couch and showed her how to lift the feet; then between us we managed to get him into the back of the car. I covered him with the blanket I had seen in the boot. I pushed the fire door closed, got Jack seated in the passenger seat and then we drove Roger home. I had been to his home a couple of times, so I knew where it was.

It wasn't long before we were turning into the lane which led up to his house. I stopped in front of the garage. Leaning over, I found the remote control in the glovebox and flashed it at the sensor. We watched in silence as the door moved slowly upwards.

'Thank you, Roger,' I thought.

He had been like a child with a new toy, and he insisted on giving me several demonstrations on how the system worked on my previous visits. I put the headlights on and drove slowly into the garage. I wanted to make sure I left enough space to open the back door. After stopping the car, I got out and operated the switch to close the door. Finding the light switch, I turned on the light. I went back to my side of the car and turned off the car's lights. I told Jack to stay where she was; then I went through the connecting door into the kitchen, then into the lounge, putting on the lights as I went. I made sure there was nothing in the way. I also pulled the curtains in the lounge. Satisfied, I went back to the garage to get Jack. Between us we managed to carry and drag Roger into the lounge. We laid him on the floor in front of the armchair where he used to sit to watch the TV. I took from my pocket the scissors I had brought and carefully snipped open my parcel. Jack stood and watched, not understanding any of this. (Not that it would matter, as I could erase it all later.) I asked her to help with the feet and we dragged him into the chair. I repositioned him a couple of times before I was satisfied. I turned to Jack and asked her to find a carrier bag.

"There's probably one in the kitchen," I suggested.

While she was gone, I carefully folded up the plastic sheet. She was soon back, and she helped me put the sheet in the bag; then I placed it by the front door. Turning to Jack, I smiled. Then, taking her arm, I steered her back into the kitchen. I asked her to fill the kettle and to find a mug and saucer. I searched the cupboards until I found the tin with the tea bags. I emptied the tin out on to a piece of kitchen towel, and from my jacket pocket I took a plastic bag which contained some of the tea bags from the lab. I opened the bag and gave a tea bag to Jack, who popped it in the mug. The rest of the bags I emptied into the tin, which I replaced in the cupboard. Roger's tea bags I put into the empty plastic bag. I asked Jack to put two sugars in the mug when she had put the water and milk in. Returning to the hall, I put the plastic bag of tea bags into the carrier bag. On my way past the kitchen I told Jack I was just popping upstairs. I soon located Roger's bedroom, and found what I wanted in the first place I looked: the top drawer of the bedside cabinet. It was a buff folder containing lots of handwritten notes. I read a few just to make sure, then I returned downstairs to where Jack was standing, patiently holding the mug of tea. I think the poor love thought it was for me. I put the folder in the carrier bag, then took the mug from her, went into the lounge and placed it on the small table next to where Roger was sitting. I tilted his head back and spooned some tea into his mouth; then from my other pocket I took another plastic bag containing biscuits from the lab. I put two of the biscuits in the saucer, while I put the bag back in my pocket; then I dunked one of the biscuits in the tea and put the soggy part into Roger's mouth. The rest of the biscuit I put in his hand on his lap. Taking Jack with me, I went back to the kitchen and opened the plastic box labelled 'pig biscuits', which had been a present from a previous girlfriend, Roger had told me. I emptied the box out, and put in the rest of the biscuits from the lab. Roger's biscuits went into the carrier bag in the hall. I told Jack to wait by the front door.

I returned to the garage and had a quick look in the car, remembering to fold the blanket and return it to the boot. Then I remembered I had moved the driver's seat forward two clicks, so I put it back in its original position. After a last look round, I switched off the light.

Back in the kitchen again, I had a last look round. I placed Roger's car keys in the dish on the fridge, as he had done the last time I visited him. The kitchen light I left on. I smiled to Jack as I passed through the hall and into the lounge. I turned on the TV and put the remote control on the arm of Roger's chair. I turned on the standard lamp behind him. I then had second thoughts about the remote control and gave it a gentle push so that it fell to the floor. Over at the door, I had a last look round, then turned the main light off. It looked such a perfect picture: a man, home after a hard day, had fallen asleep in front of the TV – a scene probably repeated in numerous households throughout the world. I walked over to Jack and picked up the carrier bag.

"Time to go, my love," I said with a smile.

Leaving the hall light on, I opened the front door and we left the house. In the lane I stopped and asked Jack to hold the carrier bag. I peeled off my surgical gloves and popped them in the bag. Taking the bag from Jack, I gave her a big smile. Then I took her arm and we walked away up the lane, just like any happy couple out for an evening stroll.

We returned to the lab, taking a bus as far as Wheyton, and then a taxi.

Sitting in my armchair, I looked round my cosy flat and realised that Roger had never been in it. I was quite proud of it really. It had once been a collection of storerooms, built on to the side of the lab. Using the remote, I energised the TV.

After a few minutes Jack came in with a tray and put a cup of tea next to me. I laughed out loud at the irony that it was almost a repeat of the scene at Roger's. Jack looked at me with surprise.

"Oh, just something that struck me as funny, my dear!"

As I sat sipping my tea, I thought of all the clever little touches. I mean, at the post-mortem if they examined his stomach contents, the tea and biscuits they would find would be the same as the ones in his house. What about the cause of death? Well, that would be heart failure. The drug I had given him (a by-product of my experiments with animals) blocked the signals from the brain which keep the heart going, so it would just stop. Oh, I know some clever clogs could probably find traces of the drug if they knew what to look for, but why would they bother? There were no suspicious circumstances, and certainly no links with me. I had already got a new identity for Jack – she was already wearing her clothes. My lady friend hadn't left in a hurry;

she was still here, buried out in the grounds, a victim of earlier research. And now I had brought her back to life, given her a new body.

It was four days later when I spotted the story in the *Tolchester News:* 'Roger Watson, a detective inspector on an exchange scheme from the Metropolitan Police, has died of a heart attack while at home. . . .'

I put the paper down and let out a whoopee! Jack came rushing in from the kitchen.

"Edward, what's wrong?"

"Oh, nothing, my dear – just a good piece of news."

I settled back into my chair. Nothing could stop me now, I thought. I started to go over in my mind the ideas that had formed over the last few days. I could live for ever. I could copy the data from my brain and put it in a new young body; then my knowledge would continue to grow. I could make millions by doing the same for other people. Parents could have their data transferred to their sons' and daughters' brains and live on in their bodies. Animals? I could produce freaks and sell them to shows – the domestic cat that behaves like a monkey! Oh, yes – I could have a hundred Jacks all in different bodies, all wanting to please me. I could become the most powerful man in the world. Just think, the man sitting next to you, sleeping next to you, could be me. How would a woman know if the man she kissed goodbye in the morning would be the same man who came home at night? He might look the same, but . . . I could offer people the chance to change their partner's mind in any way they wanted – for a price, of course. The husband could pay me to change his wife into a nymphomaniac, and pay me again not to change her back if she should ask. I could set up a data library. I could just picture it: rows and rows of brains in jars, all coupled up to computers. People could select the sort of brain they want. A sort of pick and mix!

God? Now there's a thought: why shouldn't I be a god?